SEDUCTION

A Money, Power & Sex Story

NORIAN LOVE

This is a work of fiction. Names, characters businesses, organizations, places, events and incidents are either the product of the author's imagination or used facetiously. Any resemblance to actual persons, living or dead, events or locales is entirely coincidental.

Dedicated to the Pyramids, and returning home.
NL

WHY I WROTE THIS BOOK:

An author friend of mine told me, "Everyone has at least one book inside of them—almost no one has two." It stuck with me for months. Was this something I could do, again? The voice of doubt wasn't gone, but it changed. My would-be critics were real critics now and good or bad, they would have another opinion. Maybe I should quit while I was ahead. Maybe I should forget about this. It wasn't romantic anymore. It was something else. It was work. And so, if I could attribute this book to any singular thing it would be to labor. This book is the product of such labor. It was the work that kept me going when it was all said and done. The fact that so many people start a good idea, or any idea, but aren't willing to finish it for whatever reason. Real or imaginary, we find reasons to stop doing things we were driven to do; to stop working at the things we love. It could be heartbreak, life's busywork, some urgent crisis we need to tend to, or my favorite— Netflix—something will get in the way. Someone told me the first thing you have to do to achieve your dream is wake up. Endurance became a friend, and I learned once again something very beautiful in this process: if this is what I want to do with my life, then I have to actually *do it*. So, while I romanced countless hours over the first story thinking up scandals for Nichelle to fall into, I found no such comfort in this book. This one challenged me, like life does sometimes.

Whatever your dream, there will be a point in time where you'll be tested. You can't spell *testimony* without the "test," after all. Now, looking at it in hindsight, on the eve of first print, what has been revealed to me is one simple universal truth: All things are possible if you want them to be. You just have to be willing to work at it.

Blessings,

Norian

CHAPTER 1
WELCOME TO THE VA

"Another beautiful day in Richmond, Virginia. Clear skies with a high of 78. We've had amazing weather, folks." Kendra changed the channel as she held the phone to her ear. By the fourth ring, she was highly annoyed, but still she waited on her friend until the phone picked up.

"If this heffa don't answer the damn phone!" She mumbled softly to herself, but like always, it went to voicemail. She hung up without leaving a message. She simply pushed the 'End' button angrily and tried the phone number again. Same result.

"Hi, you've reached the voicemail of Ronnie Duvalle with Burrows Industries. Please leave a message, and I will promptly return your call."

This time, Kendra accepted the invitation. "Damn it, Ronnie, it's Kendra. I know you're getting my calls. Now, give me a call back this morning. I just want to check on you."

Kendra hung up the phone. Flustered, she put the phone down and looked at the stock price of the company she worked for. It was moving north of fifteen percent in early morning trading, despite rumors of turmoil coming out of the Houston office. *What in the hell is going on?* she thought to herself as she scrolled through the rest of her portfolio. It was always soothing for her to look at her accounts. It reminded her she was doing well. It also distracted her from the other thoughts on her mind. Kendra Daniels was never a person to do well without answers. She wanted answers—no, she *needed* answers—but beyond that, she wanted in on the action. She needed to be in the action; to be in the know. That was paramount to everything else, and the action for this company was in Houston. She looked at the phone as if willing it to ring, but to no avail. She wanted to call again, but didn't want to appear desperate. There was nothing she could do but wait. She opened a draft of an email to send to Ronnie, thinking the woman would respond a bit more expediently that way when the phone rang. She looked at the caller ID: Queen Savage Bitch. She smirked at the name coded in her phone for her former rival turned friend. It was the contact name she saved when they first met each other, and she hadn't bothered to change it because, in many ways, it still fit. It was the first time she thought about it, though, since she'd moved back home to Virginia after taking an unofficial demotion after her disappointing performance in Houston. She picked up the phone and in an accusatory fashion and said, "Girl, I know you saw me calling you. Not cool, Ronnie."

"I'm sorry, Kendra, I didn't know I reported to you. I thought it was still the other way around."

"Bitch, you know we still have the same title."

"For now, but as you can tell by our soaring stock price, that's temporary. You're welcome, by the way. All the money I'm making us is sure to help in your bed-and-breakfast-slash-tour-the-Confederate-monuments business you're undoubtedly working on in that God-forsaken city."

"Ah, Ronnie, still taking your daily dose of vitamin bitch, I see."

"I miss you, too, girl."

It was their usual banter, although it always dug a little deeper than Kendra would like. Ronnie was her friend, and while she respected her skillset, she couldn't help but feel, that on a professional level, she was more qualified than her rival. It was just her competitive nature. Right now, Ronnie had the advantage. She worked in corporate headquarters, and most importantly, was delivering results. A fifteen percent upswing in the stock price meant she was making millions for shareholders, and anyone who can make the shareholders richer would get more chances to do so. Which meant Kendra's days in Virginia would be longer than she wanted. Yet, she was still proud of her friend. At this level, she was aware that there had to be solidarity among women of color—a lesson she learned the hard way while living in Houston roughly six months earlier, competing with Ronnie for the same vice presidential position. While Kendra did all she could to assert herself, and her analytical skills were second to none, Ronnie was supportive. She was the ulti- *are you? stupid.* mate team player and even covered for Kendra on occasion. That left an impression on Kendra to make sure she never competed with another sister again for a job. At least not in a way they'd tear each other down. It also exposed her insecurities. At the time, she would've done anything to belittle Ronnie, not only because she wanted the title, but because, if she were being truly honest with herself, a part of her just didn't like the woman back then. It wasn't until she was being transferred that she truly gained respect for Ms. Duvalle. — *Because you were better*

"So, are the rumors true?" Kendra insisted, cutting straight to the original intent of her call.

"The rumors?"

"Bitch, don't play with me! Tell me what is going on down there. I hear there are layoffs coming, and on top of that, the girl who took my place took a leave of absence. What was her name? Nicole?"

"Worthless was her name."

"Ronnie!"

"Nichelle. Her name was Nichelle."

"That's right... Nichelle. Myers, isn't it? Why did she leave?"

"It's such a long, sordid story, Kendra. A lot is going on, but the good news is your 401(k) will look all the better for it."

"So, that's it? Ho, I want details!"

"Kendra, it's a really long story."

"Ronnie, I'm in Richmond, Virginia. This is where time goes to die. Spill it!" She was in no mood for Ronnie's faux coyness. She knew if she were in Houston, the gossip would spill over and she'd know all the dirt—maybe even a useful tidbit or two to help her regain some leverage in the company. But even the rumor mill was slow in Richmond. There wasn't a lot she could do but wait for Ronnie to tell her what was going on.

"Okay, I'll tell you, but some of this stuff is still unfolding, so I don't have the answers to everything."

"God damn it, Duvalle!" Kendra said, frustration saturating her tone.

Ronnie finally got the hint and revealed everything that happened in the past twenty-four hours. "We had a meeting with the board. Rainhouse & Arms, the new audit firm, recommended an upgrade in technology to reach our quarterly projection. They then recommended a ten-percent reduction in workforce to exceed the quarterly fiscal projection. The board loved the idea."

"So, basically, layoffs to make more money."

"Well, in layman's terms, yes."

"Then why did Nichelle need to take a leave of absence?"

"That's much more complicated. She was upset about the workforce reduction, but—"

"Wait," Kendra interjected. "Did you say Rainhouse & Arms? I've heard that name in the news recently. Isn't that where that guy worked who is at the center of the police shooting that all the protests are about in Houston?"

"Yeah."

"Holy shit! Was he working on our account?"

"He was more than that. He's the guy I've been dating."

There was a silence on the phone. Kendra was at a loss for words and wanted her friend to say something, but what she didn't know. She was too overwhelmed by the information she just received.

"Ronnie, why didn't you lead with that?"

"Because the whole thing is a cluster fuck! I don't know. You're asking a lot from me right now."

"Damn, girl, I'm sorry. Lucas is his name, right? I saw it on the news. Is he okay?"

"He's in a comma. It's too soon to say anything, honestly. We're not sure what to make of the circumstances right now. It's really touch and go."

"What in the hell happened?"

There was more silence on the phone. Kendra's mind raced. She was concerned for her friend, but at the same time, her mind was building a stockpile of questions.

"Ronnie?"

"Lucas... he and I were having a... disagreement over something when Nichelle called."

"Hold up," Kendra interjected "This was after work, right? Why would Nichelle call him after work?"

"Because he had recently broken up with Nichelle around the time he got to the company, so they had some ten—"

"Are you fucking kidding me?"

"Stay with me, Kendra."

"This is too much. I need a drink." Kendra got up as she listened to the rest of the story. She also sensed Ronnie needed a moment to sort it all out. Her purple, laced boy shorts clinging against her milk chocolate thighs, she walked into the kitchen to pour a glass of wine. She kept a bottle of Wild Horse Cabernet for occasions like this. She poured the already-open bottle into a glass and went back to the living area where her laptop sat and glanced at the stock price. Up seventeen percent now.

"So... what happened again?" She heard a deep sigh on the other end of the line. The wounds were still fresh from the night before.

" Lucas had recently broken up with Nichelle when we met. I don't usually date men on the job, but he was different."

"I remember you said you loved him, but you failed to include he was Nichelle's ex."

"It never seemed important when we were talking. This all started around the time you were leaving town anyway."

"Right. You were going to meet him the last night we had drinks."

"I think so. I can't remember. At any rate, you had your own issues with your man. Besides, you barely remember the girl's name until now, and their past wasn't any of my business."

"Fair enough. So, how did he get shot?"

"I was about to tell you that before you decided to interrupt me for the umpteenth time."

"Sorry, but you gotta admit, this is pretty far-fetched."

"You get no argument here."

"So... how did he get shot?"

"We were having a disagreement, and Nichelle called him. They had some issues to resolve. He went over to her house, and well..."

"Let me get this straight—he got shot at Nichelle's house?"

For the first time since she knew Ronnie, Kendra sensed her vulnerability. There were echoes of what sounded like muffled sobbing followed by what was obviously a mute. She knew that Ronnie was too proud to actually cry on the phone, but the fact that she was able to let her guard down at all meant this topic was much more sensitive than Kendra had considered. Her friend's lover was in the hospital fighting for his life, and she had been treating the entire event like a soap opera. While she wanted answers, she decided the best thing to do was change the subject.

"So, when do they announce you as the queen of all Burrows Industries?"

Kendra sensed the phone unmute, followed by a sniffle and her friend's cracking voice. "I... um... I'm not sure. We're having a meeting today."

"Well, the stock is up around eighteen and a half percent. I'm sure it has to be soon."

Ronnie chuckled shakily, which made Kendra feel better "Enough of all that, girl. How's life on your end?"

"Oh, you know, the usual. Just looking at floor plans for my Confederate bed 'n' breakfast as you so eloquently put it." The two chuckled at the joke as Kendra continued. "Outside of that, I'm still dealing with Marcus's ass."

"What do you mean?"

"You remember how you thought he would go back to the way he used to be once we left Houston?"

"I do."

"Well, let's just say that plan didn't work out as well as you thought it would. I mean, don't get me wrong, he's wonderful again, but—"

"But what?"

"Something's definitely different. He's different now."

"Well, I didn't know him before, so what do you mean 'different'?"

6

"I can't really put a label on it, but if I had to say anything, I'd say it feels like he's trying too hard."

"I thought that's what you wanted."

"I wanted my Marcus back. Right now, he's hot and cold. Does that make any sense?"

"Not in the least."

Kendra took a pause. It was hard to put into words what was going on with Marcus, though she wanted to talk about it, if for nothing else than to have a healthy distraction from her newfound awareness of her friend's problems. Marcus trying too hard wasn't as bad as Ronnie's boyfriend getting shot, but it was still her problem and she wanted to get it out in the open. Since she and Marcus moved back home, she'd never actually taken the time to figure out what was bothering her. This was her opportunity to do so. She took a deep sigh and unloaded what had been eating at her for the last few months.

"The thing is, Marcus... he's lazy, unmotivated, and that shows up sometimes in the bedroom. Don't get me wrong. He has the equipment and he knows—well, knew—how to use it, but now he's just looking for a way to be done in the bedroom. Like he's spent his energy all day fucking someone else, and that's when he's not acting like he's God's gift to all women."

"Okay, now we're getting somewhere, Normally I'd say this would be too much information about your boyfriend's... um, package, but I haven't gotten any, and by the looks of things I won't be getting none anytime soon, so I'll indulge. I thought you realized you were just being paranoid when you lived down here."

"I did. Well, at least I thought so at first. I thought we'd get on that plane and life would go back to normal, but it didn't. In fact, it did the exact opposite. It felt like guilt. I mean, it wreaked of guilt. I'm convinced now that something definitely happened in Houston."

"But Houston is your past, Kendra, at least in the sense of this relationship. I have to admit it sounds like you're looking for something, anything, to justify your feelings. You don't have any concrete proof he did something wrong, or is doing anything wrong right now. And most importantly, he's trying. Don't take this the wrong way, girl, but it sounds like you're looking for a reason your career didn't work out here and not anything Marcus actually did."

The words stung, the truth behind them piercing a most vulnerable wall she hadn't bothered to defend since she was talking to her friend.

"Well, that hurt, you blunt motherfucker," she said playfully.

Ronnie laughed at her retort. "I'm sorry, girl. I just think you're worried about the wrong thing. It's not like he's—"

"Intuition."

"Excuse me?"

"Intuition. I know this man's sleeping patterns; I know his scent; I know how he lies, when he lies, why he lies. I pay attention to his eating habits, and consequently know the pattern of his bowel movements. I know when he drinks vodka he's going to pass out before he can get it up, and when he drinks Hennessey, I'm going to be laying in the room with my legs folded up in the air with my titties bouncing against my knees and my big toes touching the headboard until four a.m. I know how the bristles of his mustache feel on my pussy when he gets a fresh haircut. I know this man. In-tu-ition. It's what made me feel something was wrong when we were in Houston, it's what made me feel something isn't right since we got back from Houston, and it is certainly what's making me feel—at this very moment—something is definitely wrong."

Kendra stayed quiet, hoping her friend would fill the void. Anything would've done at the moment. Instead, the silence persisted, which only made Kendra's insecurities grow. She wanted validation from Ronnie, but knew she would get no such reprieve. Marcus, for better or worse, was her rock, her foundation, and she knew that women like Ronnie, women like the one she was pretending to be anyway, thought taking care of a man was a weakness. Yet, Kendra hoped that maybe, in light of Ronnie's own relationship woes, she'd be supportive. The awkwardness grew as no words were exchanged. Kendra was about to speak when the phone beeped. It was Burrows Industries.

"Hey, Ronnie, are you calling me from work?"

"No."

"Okay, well, hang on, girl, I gotta call you back. This is the Houston office."

"Really? That's odd. What could they possibly want?"

"I'm not sure, but I'll let you know. Let me grab the line, and I'll call you back."

"Okay."

Kendra clicked over just in time to get the line.

"Kendra Daniels."

"Hi, Kendra, this is Milton Burrows. Do you have a moment to speak?"

Ceo (President

CHAPTER 2
WHY DO YOU LIKE TO FUCK OTHER WOMEN?

well that's quite the chapter title

not Kendra! He is still cheating!

"**F**uck me harder!" the red-haired woman screamed as Marcus pushed his nine-inch rod deep into her freshly shaved vagina. He obeyed the command, thrusting deeper into her as her eyes rolled into the back of her head. Her ginger hair drenched with sweat whipped against his shoulder blades as he shoved into her against the wall. He had been at it for twenty minutes at this point. "That's it! Oh, God! Marcus, don't stop!" she yelled as she bit him *proof!* on the side of his neck. He pressed his chest against hers. He could feel her insides firming.

"Oh, fuck, I'm cumming again!" She squealed as he continued to massage her G-spot with his vessel. By his count, this was her forth orgasm, something he enjoyed since he could feel the fluid secrete from her body as she came, which, in turn, hardened his dick even more. He continued to thrust inside her, pressing her back firmly against the wall as he entered her repeatedly. Her body went limp from orgasm as he held her buttocks, never stopping his rhythm. He was close to orgasm himself. In a final thrust, he released his seed into her vagina. *Hope she on BC!*

"Oh, fuck!" he exclaimed as pleasure surged through his body with each stroke. He released the woman he was holding, and in an instant, their closeness ceased. Marcus walked over to the crème couch he had tossed his clothes on and picked them up. The woman walked over to him and wrapped her arms around his chest as she kissed him on his back.

"That was amazing!" she exclaimed, her head pressed against his back. Marcus stood silent, sensing that his silence had replaced their intimacy with tension. "Babe, something wrong?" she asked.

"I need to use your shower," he replied as he organized his clothes. The redhead walked from behind him to face him, her hair and milk-white skin glistening with sweat. "You don't want a round two?"

"No, I need to use your shower now."

"Is that Sergeant Marcus Winters giving me an order, or is this my friend Marcus asking to use my shower?"

Marcus rolled his eyes. The woman, stunned by his reaction, persisted. "What in the hell is that for?"

"Is that what we are, Elaine? Friends?"

"That's what we've always been."

"Really? 'Cause I just spent the last half hour fucking your brains out."

The woman smiled as she bit the tip of her right index finger. "Friends with benefits."

"Damn it, Elaine! You're supposed to be my counselor. This isn't counseling!"

"It is. Consider it advanced sexual therapy." The woman stroked his penis. "If we can figure out the source of your problem, we can resolve the issue, and it is my professional opinion your problem resides in this wonderful little guy right here." He removed her hand from his rod.

"I can't believe the Army pays you for this," he scoffed.

"It's funny. When you walked in my door, your dick didn't seem very concerned about my professional opinion."

"That's because it was already in your mouth."

"That's low, Marcus."

"But honest."

"You want to use my shower, fine. You know where it is."

Marcus looked down at the five-foot-seven redhead's ocean water eyes. He smirked.

"I'm tripping. I'm sorry." He grabbed her hand and walked her into the bedroom. As he did, he looked at the slate-gray walls to see if they had damaged the sheet rock, or if the paint was worn from Elaine's firm body being pressed so roughly against it. "There's a dent in your—" *there before.*

"Come on now, Sergeant Winters. This is Army you're talking to. We all have a few battle scars," she said with a wink. That was comforting to hear. Elaine wasn't anything like he remembered her when they served together. She was a lot more rigid in their military days. Then again, she was a lot more organized, as well. The two walked across the deep oak, hardwood floors to the bedroom and into the bathroom to bathe each other's scent off. For Marcus, that appeared to be it. He was silent the entire shower, a man to himself, as he concentrated on the scent of the dove soap and metal residual in the water as his lover washed his muscular golden-brown frame. He returned the favor in a groping fashion, somewhat disinterested— something Elaine picked up on, and so she took over the duties of cleaning her body herself. As she finished rinsing off, she whispered, "I'll be in the living room when you get out."

When she got out the shower, he fully embraced the water on his face as if cleansing away any wrongdoing on his part. For five minutes, he stood in the shower, the heat barely tolerable. It was painful, but a part of him felt he deserved it. As he turned off the water, he stepped through the glass doors, the steam covering the porcelain vanity sink with the stainless-steel French faucet. The walls were a gray sandstone tile, similar in color to the textured walls that ran throughout the house. She wasn't active duty anymore, and it showed. While still in the reserves, Elaine had done well for herself, making good money in the private sector. He dried off with the olive towel she left for him and slipped his basketball shorts and solid navy blue T-shirt back over his body. As he walked out, still drying his hair, he tossed the towel into the bathroom hamper.

As he scanned the bedroom, he heard his name. "Marcus, I'm in here." Marcus walked into the living room to see Elaine fully dressed in a black skirt and white blouse. Her hair, still slightly wet from a rushed blow-dry session, was tied in a bun. She completed her look with black, steel-framed glasses.

"What's this for?" he asked.

"You wanted to have a real session. I'm giving you one."

He looked around. He wasn't sure what to make of this.

"Please have a seat." she insisted. Curious, he took her up on her offer. He sat on the crème couch across from the matching loveseat Elaine currently occupied.

"Shall we begin?" she asked inquisitively.

"Yeah... I... yeah, let's begin," he said, somewhat uncertain at first, then confident. He was finally getting what he wanted: Elaine in her professional capacity.

"So, Marcus, why do you like to fuck other women?"

"What?" he exclaimed.

"Why do you like to fuck other women?"

The question hurt more that it shocked him. He didn't know how to respond.

"I don't like to sleep with—"

"Let's be clear, Marcus. This only works with complete honesty. You want to figure out what's triggering your... escapades, then you have to be totally open with me. That's the only way this will work. Understand?"

He nodded in agreement. It was what he desired, after all. He needed to get to the bottom of his problem.

"Now, having said that, you still haven't answered my question. Why do you like to fuck other women?"

"I'm... I'm not sure."

"Take a guess."

"I like pussy, Elaine. I don't know."

"Haven't you always liked pussy, Marcus? When we were in the military, I'm sure you liked pussy then, but to my knowledge— in fact, it was general knowledge—you didn't sleep around. Believe me, I know."

"What are you talking about?"

"Oh, come on, Marcus! Me, along with every other woman on that

13

base, were practically presenting our vaginas to you like medals. We were all throwing ourselves at the great Sgt. Marcus Winters. You didn't give us the time of day. We thought you might be gay until you brought your beloved Kendra to base, which made it all the more exciting for us. We even had a running bet; a monthly pot. The women of Bravo Company each put fifty dollars in to see who'd be the first to screw you. The first person to get a confirmed kill, meaning a blowjob, handjob, taking it up the ass, or whatever way you liked it, got the cash." wow.

"Is that what you guys were doing? I thought you were playing bingo or something." wow

"We were playing Fuck the Sarge! And everyone lost... well, except me now. That pot was pretty high, too. We all ended up giving the money back. Damn it, I wonder if I could call up the girls now and get them to pony up. Ahhh, it won't matter—they won't believe me."

"This is crazy. You were directly in my chain of command. There was no way I was ever going to sleep with any of you."

"That's what I thought at first. I said here's a man who bleeds for the flag, a true patriot. As soon as you were discharged, though, I sought you out. But no, you were in a relationship and seemed even happier than you were in the service. I thought there was no way I'd ever get a chance to be with you. It was Kendra this and Kendra that. You were even going to marry her. So, what changed?"

"I'm not sure what changed," he barked defensively.

"Okay, if you don't know what changed, tell me when you felt it changed. At least in your mind, for you."

He took a deep breath. He wanted a drink, but realized that drinking is what put him in his current situation. It's what led to him sleeping with Elaine Holt the former military counselor. He needed to answer the question, but didn't have a clue where to begin.

"Let's do this—tell me about the first time you slept with another woman that wasn't Kendra."

This question was a lot easier. Something he could dive into.

"And this is all confidential, right? I'm paying you for this to be confidential."

"Marcus, despite what we're doing, yes, this is confidential. I am your friend, but I take my job very seriously."

He nodded and decided to tell his story.

"Okay, I can do that. It was in Houston. We had been down there for a few months, and every day Kendra would come back overwhelmed by the job, but even more stressed out about this coworker of hers. Every night, she was in no mood to have sex, and she was gone first thing in the morning. And it was a big problem for me, since we used to have sex all the time. At first, I was understanding, but after a while, I got frustrated. Then, one day—not sure exactly when—but we had just had a huge argument about sex. It wasn't long after Kendra left that this beautiful, light-skinned woman rang the doorbell smelling like heaven. She asked if I was Marcus. I said yes, and she pulls off her coat. She's wearing nothing but a black bra and black panties. She said 'I'm here to fuck you.' I had never seen this woman before. It was like something out of a movie. She was beautiful. I mean, really beautiful. She walked in and began to take my clothes off right there. I didn't stop her because, hell, I wanted it. I needed to have sex at that point. I was jacking off like I'd brush my teeth in the morning. The sex was amazing. I mean, even if I was getting it every day, I wasn't getting it like this. So, that changed things. When we were done, I asked her what her name was. She told me it was Ronnie. She was cool—much different than Kendra. We started hooking up from time to time, and each time my mind would be blown. But I never knew how she found me until one night Kendra starts going on about the coworker that's giving her hell. She'd always say 'This savage bitch at work,' or the '*Queen Savage Bitch*' when she was referring to her. This time she called her by her real name: Ronnie. Come to find out I was just a pawn in the whole thing. Ronnie used me to throw Kendra off her game, and it worked. As soon as we found out Kendra was being transferred back to Richmond, Ronnie told me, in no uncertain terms, she didn't want shit to do with me. I felt terrible. I thought I'd come back here and try to be the best boyfriend I could be. Try to find a job and get married, but for all the wrong that was done, Ronnie had woken something up in me. It was like a light switch. I—"

"I'll stop you right there, Marcus. That's an amazing story. So, when you got back to Richmond, you said you tried to be the best boyfriend you could be, but you still slept with other women. Why do you think that's the case?"

"I guess I realized that women wanted me and appreciated who I was already. The way Kendra used to, and well... I guess that's why I slept with them."

"It sounds like Kendra's standards for you have changed. Does she have higher standards now?"

"Yes... no... I mean, kind of. Man, I don't know. The military is all about discipline. It's easy. You follow orders, do as you're told—but outside the military, it's anyone's guess. Before she took the job in Houston, the plan was clear. Get a job and get married. Then, start a family. But when she got down there, she started talking about being a power couple. My not finding a job was getting in the way of some master plan she concocted."

"She made you feel inferior."

"She didn't make me feel like a man, that's for sure. Everything was, 'Marcus, I need you to do this,' 'Marcus, go get that for me.' When I complained, she would remind me how she was carrying us. That pissed me off."

He sat while Elaine took notes on his life. He was somewhat uncomfortable with his therapist also being his side piece, but it felt good to get it off his chest.

"Elaine, can I just say that—"

"I'm afraid that's all we have time for today." He was stunned. He wasn't sure how to respond.

"Excuse me?"

"Well, you made it perfectly clear you wanted to keep the boundaries of our personal and professional lives separate. Since you're paying me for an hour, time is up. Now, if you want to slide that nice, long, caramel dick into any orifice on my body, I'd be more than willing to oblige, but as a professional, I'm off the clock." WTF?!

He sat, looking at her stunned, and shaking his head.

"You're something else, you know that?"

"That is precisely the point. Our hour of therapy is over, and I'm now something else. Which means, Marcus, I can be anything you want me to be right now."

She stood up from the loveseat and slowly unbuttoned her shirt, revealing that she hadn't bothered to put on a bra after their previous session. Marcus, a bit agitated by the circumstances, stood up and searched for his car keys.

"Marcus, what are you doing?"

"Hour's up, and I'm heading home. Peace, Elaine."

now you got standards? Humph!

CHAPTER 3
MR. BURROWS

"Mr. Burrows, to what do I owe the pleasure of this call?" Kendra asked. It was unexpected, considering everything going on in Houston. She thought the president of the company had better things to do with his time than call her.

"Ms. Daniels, I'll get straight to the point. We want you to consider coming back to the Houston office."

"Houston?"

"Yes. Will that be a problem? Because—"

"Not a problem, just a surprise."

It was a bombshell. The man was still talking, but she'd all but stopped listening after those words. Houston was where she wanted to be. The answer was yes. But she didn't want to appear too desperate, and her pride was a little dinged from being transferred back to Richmond initially, so a simple 'yes' wasn't happening. "It's kind of a surprise, Mr. Burrows."

"Milton. Mr. Burrows is my father."

"Okay... Milton. It's kind of a surprise, and to be honest, since I've been back, I'm actually getting into a nice groove here in Richmond. I've assembled a good team, and I don't want to let them down."

"We've taken notice. That is precisely why we want you to come back. I know things didn't go as expected last time, but you're a talented woman, and the company is moving in stratospheric directions. We want to show strength, and we need our best and brightest in the heart of the company. You are one of the best and brightest. We want you—no, we need you—to come to Houston."

It was bullshit, and she knew it was bullshit, but it felt so good to hear. Milton was, if nothing else, a charmer. The truth of the matter is it didn't matter what he had to say. A chance to go back to Houston would mean she could get her career back on track. It also meant she'd once again be going head to head with her friend, Ronnie Duvalle. Most importantly, it meant that Ronnie was, in fact, not getting the promotion she'd been hoping for, yet again. That, in itself, was a curious thing, considering Ronnie had done everything right, at least on the surface. Kendra wanted to pry without ruffling any feathers, so she decided to play oblivious and ask indirectly, "So, does this mean you want me to come back to do my old job?"

"Yes."

"Does that mean I'll be reporting to Ms. Duvalle?"

"Things are pretty fluid at the moment. The important thing is to get you down here."

Milton played things pretty close to the vest, but his ambiguous answer was all but a definite no. Ronnie was not getting promoted. Kendra was relieved, though a part of her felt guilty. She wanted her friend to succeed, considering all she'd been through, but not at the cost of her own career. It was hard, but it was business. Still, none of it made sense as the stock price was soaring.

"I've also heard rumors of lay—"

"Let me stop you there, Kendra. We don't want to invest too much energy in speculation or water-cooler gossip. The important thing now is to get you down to Houston should you decide to take the job."

She wanted to say yes right away, but still hesitated. A yes right now would reek of desperation, and she felt she could at least get a raise out of delaying her answer. Also, there was Marcus. She didn't even think to consider him while plotting her return. Would it impact their relationship like last time? She just wasn't sure if they could survive another chance to live in Houston.

"I'm truly honored you would consider me. I would like some time to think this over if that's okay."

"I was actually going to recommend the same thing. There are still a lot of moving parts. Let's get back together in, say, two or three weeks and talk about it. Agreed?"

"Sounds good to me."

"Goodbye, Kendra."

She hung up the phone and screamed with excitement. She wanted to share the news, but then became sullen. Sharing with Ronnie would mean she'd have to let her know she wasn't getting the promotion, a fact the company may not have revealed to her yet. Sharing with Marcus could lead to an argument, and she was too excited to argue. Now was a time to celebrate and enjoy being on her way back to the top of the corporate ladder. She walked over to the kitchen to open up a new bottle of Wild Horse Cabernet Sauvignon. "What do they say in Houston? It's goin' down!" she exclaimed as she opened the bottle.

"What's going down?" A voice from out of nowhere startled her. Marcus was standing near the kitchen in his blue Nike basketball shorts and white sleeveless T-shirt that exposed his muscular build.

"Oh, hey, honey, you scared me. I didn't know you were back. How was the gym?"

"It was cool. So, what were you saying just now?" Kendra ignored the question as she poured herself a glass of wine and took a gulp.

"Oh, nothing. Just thinking how much... I miss you." She walked over to him to kiss him, one which he halfheartedly returned. As she kissed him, she noticed he didn't have an odor, which was odd for him considering he had been at the gym for the last couple of hours.

"Light workout today?" she inquired.

"Huh? Oh, yeah. No, I showered at the gym."

"Oh, okay." *Bullshit,* she thought. His body was clean, and there was no odor on his clothes. Even if he showered at the gym, his clothes would still smell like he'd be working out. Instead, there was nothing. A faint perspiration, but nothing that justified two hours at the gym. Particularly the way Marcus worked out when he went. She wanted to press the issue, but decided to leave it alone for the moment. At least until she could put together more than conjecture.

"You want a glass of wine?"

"Nah, I'm good, ma. Thanks. I brought you something to eat, though."

"What's that?"

"Catfish nuggets from Mamma J's."

He handed her the bag, and she began to blush.

She loved Mamma J's. It was one of the best soul-food restaurants in Richmond. The place was literally always packed. This is why the meal was so thoughtful. She enjoyed eating there, but getting in and out of the restaurant was a hassle. It was very thoughtful of him to get her favorite snack—too thoughtful. *So, let me get this straight: yo' ass went to the gym and then went twenty-five minutes out of your way to Mamma J's, then waited God knows how long just to get some catfish nuggets for me? This shit ain't adding up.* "Must've been a short workout," she said, squinting her eyes at him, fishing for an answer to the question.

"What's that supposed to mean, KD?"

"Nothing."

She watched him as he continued to down his energy drink. The excitement of her phone call seemed like a distant memory at this moment. Right now, she was fighting the urge not to go off on this man. As he walked away, he dropped his energy drink on the floor and grabbed his shoulder. Fake!

"Marcus, baby, are you okay?"

"Yeah, I'm... fine. I'm not sure what just happened. My muscles are really tense for some reason. I guess I didn't drink enough water. I'm gonna go soak in the tub."

It wasn't like him to cramp up from exercising. He was a military man, and was in great shape. *Maybe he really did go to the gym*, she thought to herself. Looking at him in visible pain, she suddenly felt bad for thinking otherwise. "I'll run some water for you, baby."

"No, I got it. Just eat and relax," he responded.

Still, she followed him as he headed into the bedroom. *Maybe he did a light workout and went and ate on his own*, she thought to herself. She wanted to justify his time. He was an adult, after all. He didn't have to be precisely where he said he was at every moment, but he was also a military man, and routine and precision were things that didn't leave a soldier. She watched him as he turned on the water. She looked for the Epsom's salt and poured it in.

"So, were you on the phone when I came in? I thought I heard you talking to someone."

"Oh, yeah. It was just work."

"Really? What's going on?"

"Nothing. Take off your clothes, and I'll put them in the wash for you."

"Okay, that works. Thanks."

She didn't want to approach the idea of going back to Houston just yet. Marcus had made it abundantly clear he didn't want any parts of Houston, and she agreed months ago—back when the possibility seemed unrealistic. She believed she'd never get this opportunity again. But since things had changed, she figured she'd ease into the conversation after putting some feelers out. As the water level rose, he got into the tub. As he relaxed, she decided to get a pulse on the situation.

"Yeah, nothing major going on at work."

"Okay, but you said that already."

"Oh, did I?"

"What's going on, KD?" She could tell he was slightly irritated.

"I said nothing. It's not like they asked me to come back to Houston or anything."

He went silent. *Fuck, he's upset.* She wanted to avoid the conversation, but she knew he wasn't going to let this go. She expected him to respond, but instead, he relaxed even more.

"Marcus? I was just—"

"You know what, KD, do you. I hope you get everything your coveted job offers you."

"It's not like that. I—"

"It doesn't even matter. Like I said—do you."

She was upset at his nonchalant attitude. Maybe she had gone too far, but the fact he seemed unfazed bothered her.

"Why can't we talk about this as adults?"

"We could, but it seems like you already made your decision. Not like you factored me into any of it, and why should you? It's not like I put my whole life on hold for you or anything."

Says the cheater

"That's low, Marc—"

"I'm about to chill, Kendra. I've had a long day. We can talk later."

He picked his white Beats and put them in his ear. Kendra rolled her eyes and resumed getting his clothes in frustration. She grabbed his shorts and shirt and piled them, along with the rest of the clothes, in the basket. She walked to the wash area right outside the bathroom near the garage. "He won't even hear me out," she mumbled to herself. "Like I want to sit around here eating catfish nuggets for the rest of my life. It's not like his business plan is working out. I mean, someone's gotta make money around here." She continued her conversation aloud. She got to the wash area and violently separated the clothes. As she sorted the clothes, she sniffed his gym shorts. "No odor at all? That ain't adding up." She separated the basketball shorts from his boxers.

Her eyes widened. "What in the hell?"

A long, stringy, single sliver of red hair was directly on her lover's underwear. oop!

CHAPTER 4
WHOSE RED HAIR IS THIS?

What in the hell is she thinking? Houston? Again with that shit? Please! Marcus thought as he washed his skin again to properly remove any residual evidence of his previous sexual encounter. He didn't want to be anywhere near Houston, but more importantly, he didn't want Kendra anywhere near Ronnie. He was over his head in infidelity, and although he didn't want to be exposed, the fact that everything changed when Ronnie was in their lives was the real issue. Over the months, Kendra had become closer to Ronnie than he thought possible, but he knew Ronnie's true nature: cold; calculating. He tried to warn Kendra in general ways, but never too direct since he didn't want her to make a direct connection between his first indiscretion and her newfound friend. Over time, he decided that since Ronnie had gotten what she wanted, there was no way she would say anything to Kendra. Still, going back to Houston could jeopardize that.

But that wasn't the only reason he wanted to stay in Richmond. He liked his life here. There was familiarity and friends, not to mention a rent-free home he'd paid off thanks to getting a G.I. Bill loan. If he was going pick up the pieces of his own life, it had to start in Richmond. It was time for Kendra to sacrifice for him. *think she already did bro*

Ding! The phone buzzed.

He picked up his Android Phone and looked at it. There was a message from Elaine.

Another therapy session soon? There was a heart emoji next to the message.

He smiled. *This freak can't get enough.*

OK cool. Ya boy could use some more counseling, he responded.

Why no emoji? She responded back

Cause I'm not a sissy. He was against men using emojis.

Army strong huh?

Damn straight.

OK well Sergeant my orifice... Excuse me "office" is always open.

He chuckled as he locked the phone.

"Marcus, what in the hell is going on?" He jumped, startled to find Kendra so close.

Oh, shit! How long was she standing there? Did she see me smile at that message? What is she talking about? Come on, Winters, play it cool.

"Excuse me?" he replied, uncertain about the nature of her question. He didn't have to wait long to find out.

"Whose red hair is this?"

"Huh?"

"I found this piece of hair on top of your boxers, and since it can't possibly be mine and it can't be yours, we have a serious fucking problem. So, I'll ask again—whose red hair is this?"

Holy shit. Well, at least she isn't thinking about the phone. Alright Winters, you got this.

"How the hell should I know? It was on my gym clothes. It could be anyone who was working on the equipment before I got there."

"It was in your boxers, Marcus! On your boxers!"

"Man, KD... there are a hundred ways that could've happened. In fact, as I think about it, there was a dude in the gym who was slimy and all over the equipment. That's why I didn't work out hard. He had red hair. It had to come from him." He could tell she wanted to believe him, but she didn't. He'd become so good at bald-face lying that it just seemed part of the ritual. He figured it was best to not say anything more until she said something.

She squinted her eyes. He decided to get out of the tub in case she *who dat?*

decided to go Lynn Whitfield and drop a toaster in the water. Kendra wasn't a violent woman, but he didn't want to take a chance. As he stepped out and grabbed a towel, she remained silent. Against his better judgment he decided to speak.

"Kendra?"

"You're hiding something, Marcus. I can feel it. It might not be anything with this red hair, but you're doing something, and it all started the day we got to Houston."

"Oh, here we go. Is this your way of trying to change the subject about you wanting to move back there?"

"What? No—"

"'Cause everything was just fine before you mentioned the word Houston. Now, all of a sudden, I'm hiding something when you're the one with secrets."

"What do you mean?"

"What was your work call about?"

"Huh? Marcus, don't turn this on me."

"I'm not turning it—you're the one acting like everything was fine, but you knew as soon as you said anything about Houston I wasn't feeling it."

"And why aren't you feeling Houston? What aren't you telling me?"

"There's nothing to tell, Kendra. I don't like the city, but you can't seem to understand that. They offered you a job, didn't they?"

"It's not about that."

"It is to me! Now, did they, or did they not, offer you a job?"

She was silent. It was all the confirmation he needed. He walked into the other room and to pick out clothing. He found a navy blue Under Armour muscle shirt and black basketball shorts. He noticed her walk into the bedroom out the side of his eye.

"When do they want you to leave?"

"I haven't taken the—"

"When do they want you to leave, KD?"

"A couple of weeks."

He found his deodorant and put it on, then walked over to the TV. He turned it on and started to search for the episode of *Law & Order: Special Victims Unit* he recorded earlier.

"So, you're not going to say anything?"

"You know, if I did, would it make a difference? See, I understand marching orders. I understand being deployed. But this isn't that. You have a choice, and you chose Houston, so as far as I'm concerned, you're on deployment. 'Cause no way in hell I'm going down there."

"Then what about us? How are we going to survive and be together?"

"Is that what you really want? To survive and be together?"

There was silence. He fiddled with the remote control with increasing agitation. He made no eye contact with his lover. Finally, she spoke, jumping in before his show came on and he had another reason to ignore her.

"I can't do this anymore with you, pretending that everything is okay when it's not. I'm not okay, Marcus. We are not okay. I don't feel anything when we're together anymore. You and me against the world is what you promised me!"

"And I would've given you that, Kendra, but you didn't and do not want to sacrifice. You don't feel you have to. As soon as I left the military, I proposed to you, and you didn't say I do. You wanted your career to get off the ground. You didn't want to be my wife!" Oop!

She was silent again, until she walked over to the flat-screen Samsung 65-inch TV and turned it off with her hand. He could tell she was hurt and upset.

"You want to know the truth? I'd be Sergeant Marcus Winters' wife a thousand times over. I made a mistake not agreeing to marry you the first time you proposed. I thought we'd have time. But when you asked me again, I did avoid it, and it was intentional because I didn't want to be the wife of a man who had plans and can't follow through with them. Whose business plans were all just speculation and nothing real. The truth is, I didn't want to be the wife of the man standing in front of me right now."

Marcus placed both hands over his face in frustration and let out a giant sigh. She was right, and it hurt him to the core. It was time to return fire.

"You don't have to remind me that I've changed every chance you get, Kendra. I'm not the only one who's changed. You remember when

27

we first started dating? You were so shy, so insecure. You had those large braces on your teeth, unsure about anything but numbers. Pre-Cal Ken—that was your nickname in college. You were good at math, and that's all you were known for. But I saw more in you. I went out of my way to start dating you, and when we got together, you were good to me, so I was good to you. I got you into the gym. I taught you how to shop for clothes that looked nice on you. I taught you how to be confident because I was a leader. Hell, I was great to you. Do you remember that?"

. "I remember," she said quietly. "I thought all the time how lucky I was to be with you. I *wanted* to be with you. I thought, 'Here I am with a great black man. A man with vision; a man with purpose. He will love me, and I will follow him.' You were supposed to be something special, Marcus, but you never lived up to that potential."

"Potential? When in the hell did I have time, Kendra? Between your school, your career, catering to your every need, getting you in shape, moving to Houston for you, building your future—hell, building you!—when was there time? You want to make it seem like we were in this together, but the truth is, there was never an us. I had plans, lots of them after the Army, and the state of Texas was never in those plans. But I delayed those plans—my plans—for you. I delayed my life for you. I went on the back burner, and that's the real problem. Were you ever invested in me, or were you just hoping I'd turn into something because you forgot about me? That's where we lost us." She began to well up from the brutal honesty in his cross-examination.

"I put all that energy into you, and I never looked back, Kendra. I said I would love you, and I did. I loved you hard. I nurtured you; cared for you. I built your self-esteem, and what did I get in return? Not a damn thing! Nothing at all. You didn't even want me to keep this house. The one thing I worked my ass off to pay off and own, you wanted me to—"

"Oh, Lord, here we go. This god damn house again! You know what? I'm so sick and tired of this argument. Did you show me what a carrot was? Sure. You might have taken me to the gym, but it was my dedication that got the results. And as far as moving goes, I only wanted you to sell this house so we could buy something nicer when we got to Houston. There was no ulterior motive."

"I didn't want anything nicer, and I definitely didn't want anything in Houston! Why can't you get that? I put my time, my blood, my sweat, and my tears into this house. I literally took a bullet for this house we're standing in. I built the fence in the back with my own two hands. I installed the kitchen sink and the cabinets, and mounted this TV, and I didn't owe anyone a dime. And together we could've done anything we wanted, but I couldn't even have the one thing in my life I truly earned. Not if I wanted this relationship. So, it don't matter if you found a red hair or not. At the end of the day, you were not satisfied with me!"

"Is that what you think, Marcus?"

"That's what I know. Look how ungrateful you sound right now. I didn't introduce you to carrots, but I made your salads, your breakfast, and your dinners every day. I poured into you, and it just feels like you've forgotten that. So, maybe you should just forget me."

"And what's that supposed to mean?"

"I'm saying maybe it's time we start looking at things the way they've always been. You look out for you, and I look out for me."

"Again, what does that mean?"

"I think we need to go our separate ways." *The guilt is killing him. Wont a man turn it on you?*

CHAPTER 5
SAINT MARTIN (FUCK 'EM, GIRL)

"I'll go to the gym," Kendra said to herself. She'd been gone from home all day. That was the last place she wanted to be because of the silence. Kendra thought a lot about the things Marcus said the night before. Things he never really verbalized. She wanted to say something to him, but she couldn't. Silence was the loudest noise there was when it came to their arguments. Their arguments were always the worst because the silence was deafening. Neither one of them wanted to apologize, although had she been honest with herself, she understood his plight. Marcus did do a lot to help her become the woman she is today. She never wanted him to feel discredited for that. Yet, the past was the past. Maybe she hadn't been understanding enough to help him get on his feet. Maybe she had become selfish in nature. It wasn't her intent. The only thing she ever wanted was for him to reach his true potential, which was why she supported him once he left the military. Fighting in Afghanistan was hard, and she felt he deserved a bit of breathing room to move on to the next phase of his life.

But his focus never materialized. Instead, what was born out of her support was failed business venture after failed business venture and a pile of excuses a mile high. Life was hard, but it was equally hard for everyone. The Marcus she knew, the one she fell in love with, would have easily shrugged off the disappointments life had to offer. That Marcus would've kicked life's ass by now because he was a fighter. This wasn't the same man—not by a long shot.

If he had taught her anything, it was that going to the gym was a great way to relieve frustration. It had become pretty clear he was dissatisfied with her healthy habits as of late, and yesterday's tirade had her feeling more than a little insecure. Had they really broken up? Was this the end? Could she save her relationship if she didn't go to Houston? Was it even a relationship worth saving? Regardless, a good hour at the gym would put everything in order. As she got to the gym, her iPhone 7 rang. *Queen Savage Bitch* again. Kendra smiled.

"Ho, what do you want?" she fired off to her friend.

"I'm sorry, is your momma on the phone?"

"Not my momma, but I did read my horoscope, and it said I should expect a call from a thot today. It was right. Amazing how accurate those things are."

"No, see, you read your ho-a-scope. They don't even give them out to quality women. Your legs have to be open like a late-night drive-thru to even get one."

"Ho-a-scope, huh? Very clever. So, you must be a founding member?"

"Since 1997."

They both laughed. These days, it was always good to hear from Ronnie.

"So, what's going on, Kendra?"

"Girl, life has been a mess since yesterday."

"What did he do now?"

"Bitch, don't presume to know me like that! You don't even know. It could be anything."

"Is this about Marcus?"

Kendra stayed silent, so her friend continued.

"I can feel you smirking through the phone, Kendra."

"Alright, damn yes, it's about Marcus! But I—"

"You're over there acting like it I haven't been on stake-outs with you looking like we're the stars of *True Detective: Ratchet Love*. It's always about Marcus."

"Very funny."

"So what is it now? Your intuition again?"

"Well, it started out that way, but it turned into something else. I think we broke up."

"What happened?"

"It started after I got off the phone with you yesterday. Milton called and wants me to consider coming back to Houston, and then Marcus came home. He heard the conversation—well, a piece of it anyway. I found a red hair—"

"Wait, what?"

"I think we broke up—"

"No, start over. Milton called you?"

"Oh, yes. So, when we got off the phone yesterday, Milton was on the other line."

That's interesting. What did he have to say?"

Kendra, in her haste, realized she didn't want to share this information with Ronnie. It was careless of her to even bring it up. She decided to downplay the conversation.

"He told me some bullshit about best and brightest, yada yada."

"Why would he call you to relay that? There clearly had to be more to this, girl."

"I mean, it wasn't a big deal at—"

"Kendra, I know after all we've been through you're not hiding things from me now."

She had a point. Ronnie had always been there for her. She decided it was time to come clean.

"No, girl, it's not like that at all. It wasn't that big a deal. I mean, we talked, but nothing definitive... Bottom line is, he wants me to come back to the Houston office."

There was a long pause. Kendra started to get the sense that maybe the phone dropped the signal. "Ronnie, you there?"

"I'm here. Think I was in a dead zone. But that's... amazing news! When do you have to make a decision by?"

"Two weeks or so."

"Oh, you're going to love reporting to me."

It was Kendra's turn to remain silent—something Ronnie immediately picked up on.

"Unless... you know something I don't know. Was there more to your conversation?"

"Ronnie, I—"

"Kendra... no secrets."

"I didn't want to talk about this, at least not like this. He made it pretty clear I was going to get my old job back. I don't think they have any intentions on promoting you."

"He did, huh? What did he say exactly?"

"It's not what he said, it was more what he didn't say. He told me I'd be getting my old job back and everything else was uncertain."

For a third time, there was silence on the phone. Kendra knew this wasn't the information Ronnie wanted to hear. She wanted to, in some way, be supportive of her when Ronnie finally said something.

"Well, at least we get to work together again. That's for the time I'm here."

"What do you mean?"

"To be honest, I'm not even sure if I'm going to stay at this firm, girl." Kendra knew that was bullshit. Ronnie was a lifer. She entertained her because she could sense the bruises on her ego through the phone.

"What? I thought you were a lifer."

"Well, I got a lot going on in my life right now. With layoffs and Lucas being shot, I think it might be time to try something different, that's all. When you really think about it, who wants to work at a company whose first idea is to lay off a bunch of hard-working employees for profit? There's just a human element there that they lack sometimes. But let's not talk about that. You think Marcus will be on board for coming back?"

"Well, that's the point I was getting to. When I told him, he was livid. Girl, I really think me and Marcus just broke up."

"What do you mean?"

"It was crazy. I accused him of cheating; he denied it. We argued; it escalated. I told him about the job in Houston, and then it really escalated. He hasn't really said much since the conversation."

"Again, Kendra, you have—"

"I know, I know, I have to let it go. I don't know what's wrong with me. I just need to get out of here. Maybe I should come to Houston early."

"Kendra, I'm saying this as your friend—you don't need to come down here and start working immediately. You're not really good at multitasking with dick on the brain. If you and Marcus are officially over, you need to grieve this relationship. You don't want to come down here and have any residual feelings affecting your work. The last thing you need is to have a repeat performance of the last time you lived here."

Those words made sense. It was her emotions that got the better of her the last time she was in Houston. She certainly wanted to make sure there was no trace of that performance.

"I get what you're saying, girl. So, what do you think I should do?"

"Girl, go on a vacation. Get out of the city. Hell, get out of the country. I hear Saint Martin is great this time of year."

Kendra had to admit that a vacation sounded wonderful; an island paradise sounded even better.

"Saint Martin?"

"Yes, girl, go there. Drink, dance, let someone push your legs back. Have a good time."

The more she thought about it, the more sense it made. A vacation was overdue, and this was the perfect time to go.

"You know I went there once with Marcus years ago, and—"

"Girlfriend, will you quit talking about Marcus! He's old news now. Listen, you are a beautiful, intelligent, successful black woman with a purpose. You're a goddamn unicorn sitting on a pussy made of rainbows and horseshoes! And he wants to break up with you? If you ask me, I say fuck 'em, girl."

"Fuck 'em?"

"Yes, fuck 'em, girl. Fuck him! Go to Saint Martin and get your groove back. Let one of those Caribbean Mandingo's drill a hole in your back and then come down here and be the Kendra Daniels everyone heard so much about. Show them why you are the best and brightest this company has to offer."

The words of her friend inspired so much confidence in her, and the logic was hard to argue. *She wants you to die in a plane crash out there stupid*

"You know what, Ronnie? You're damn right. Fuck 'em, I'm going to Saint Martin!"

"Now that's what the hell I'm talking about. Time to use some of that black-girl magic. Get your swagger back."

Her friend could make her feel more confident than she was, and it was refreshing. Marcus hadn't done that in years. Kendra decided to postpone her gym visit and head home to pack and tell Marcus she was taking a trip.

"Girl, I'm going to get off this phone, give Marcus a piece of my mind, and book this flight."

"Now, as much as I'd like to believe you, you're a sucker for this dude."

"I am."

"So, girl, you'll forgive me when I say I don't believe you. You're gonna melt when you see him."

"Ronnie, not only am I not going to melt, I'm going to forward my itinerary to you. I'm booking this trip!"

"Mmm-hmm, we'll see."

"Bitch, I gotta go."

"I already told you, ya momma isn't on the phone."

They laughed again, before Ronnie took a softer tone.

"In all seriousness, girlfriend, if you get cold feet, just remember all the hell this man has put you through. You deserve a trip."

"Thanks, Ronnie. I'm glad I have someone like you in my corner. I'm glad you got my back."

"You know it. It's what we have to do."

Kendra climbed in her car and drove toward the house. She thought about all of it. Ronnie was right—she needed to get away. But she wished she could take Marcus with her. Maybe they could make up.

She pulled into the driveway and parked her Blue Lexus IS, then walked in front of the freshly cut yard Marcus had apparently been working on since she left. She wondered what she was going to say to him. There wasn't much more beyond what was said last night. Still, she wanted to get her thoughts off her chest.

She opened the door to see him sitting on the couch, watching *Law & Order: SVU* yet again. She didn't hesitate. She walked over to the TV and muttered to herself, *"Rainbow pussy, you got this!"* as she powered off the TV.

"We need to talk."

"You're still going to Houston, right?"

"I'm going to follow my dreams if that's what you're asking."

"Then there's not much to talk about."

He used the remote to turn the TV back on. His words were like a gut punch taking all the wind out of her sails. She was emotionally defeated, but she wasn't going to give up so easily. All the strength she had built up on the phone with Ronnie was a distant memory now. She turned the TV off again to gain his attention.

"Marcus, about us taking some time out?"

"I think that's a great idea."

"Well, I'm not so sure of it. I was going to take a getaway. Nothing major, but you can come to Saint Martin with me. Maybe we can work on our—" bad choice of words

"Are you serious?" he said sarcastically. "You think you're going to take me down to the islands and convince me I should move to Houston with you? I don't think so, KD. Thanks, but I'll pass."

"Why are you being an ass right now?"

He stood up from the couch and looked at her. "You think you're the shit, don't you? Like, in your mind, all your success was your own. I'm supposed to drop what I'm doing and follow you around the country because you make six figures? Let me let you know something that may come as a shock to you—I met a chubby, awkward girl with braces, and I built her into the woman you see in front of the mirror every day for no other reason than I saw her potential. So, you can act as if you are on top of the world and climbed there all by yourself, but you'll always just be Pre-Cal Ken to me."

His tone, the coldness in his eyes, the stiffness in his body, hurt her deeply. She wanted to say something, anything, that would hurt him

"You're a loser, Marcus! All you have is your past! You have nothing now. You can't even feed yourself. I do that for you. So, yeah, you're coming to Houston because if the Army doesn't take care of you, I take care of you. God knows you don't know how to take care of yourself!"

She instantly regretted her words. She wanted to apologize, but it was too late. Her phone buzzed in the middle of their awkward silence. She picked it up.

"I don't even believe this shit. We're in an argument, and you're checking work calls?"

"It's not work, it's Ronnie." She watched as his eyes widened in a peculiar way.

"What's that look about?"

"I'm just... stunned. It's even more unbelievable. You couldn't stand this girl, and now you talk to her more than you do me."

"'Cause, believe it or not, she actually gives a damn about me."

"I'm sure she does now," he retorted

"What's that supposed to mean?"

"Nothing."

He picked up his car keys as she composed her thoughts and emotions.

"Listen, KD, you do what you feel is best. I'm out. If I don't see you before your trip, it's been real."

"Marcus, where are you goi—"

"I'm going someplace to take care of myself." He walked toward the front door, not looking back until her phone buzzed again. He held on to the door knob as she checked the message.

"Is that work?"

"You seemed very concerned about who I'm on the phone with, but not concerned enough to have a real conversation with me."

"I... just want to know who is texting you so late."

"I'm sure it's still Ronnie."

"What does she want?"

"I haven't read the message."

"Just seems odd you and her sharing so much with each other."

"Let me get this straight—you don't have time to talk to me about salvaging this relationship, but you have time to talk to me about my relationship with Ronnie?"

"I... it's... it's all of it, KD. You just don't get it. I don't even care about your friendship with her. I just don't like how you have changed. Whatever. I'm out."

He walked out the door, slamming it while she sat on the olive-colored microfiber couch, tears rolling from her face.

As she wiped the tears away, her phone buzzed. She looked at the incoming text message: *Queen Savage Bitch.*

Did you book the flight? And before you lie note I'll call the office tomorrow and see where you are.

She smirked. Ronnie was persistent, if nothing else.

Not yet girl.

Life is too short to spend waiting. My lover has been shot. I can't go on vacation. You need to go. Do this for you, girl.

It was all she needed to hear. She opened her Flight Finder app and looked for the departure flight that would give her enough time to pack her things. After she confirmed the flight, she shared the data with her friend.

Flight 1284 tomorrow @ 1:25

Now get packed. And get some rest. And remember... Fuck 'em girl!

Kendra smiled. She moved from her inbox into her contacts folder. She located contact *Queen Savage Bitch* and replaced it with *Ronnie*.

"Fuck 'em, girl," she said to herself.

CHAPTER 6
MY OFFICE HOURS ARE FROM 9 TO 5

"Ungrateful motherfucker," Marcus muttered as he sped down the highway in his black Toyota Tacoma. He punched the steering wheel a moment later, barely able to contain his anger. He thought about how bold she had been to come into the living room and turn off the TV, and how she ordered him to move to Houston because he was unable to support himself. "What, I'm not a man? You just gonna cut off the TV like I'm some little kid? Fuck you!" he shouted to no one in particular.

Everything upset him. The way she pointed out either she or the Army had to support him. The fact she was going to Saint Martin. The fact he couldn't afford to go to Saint Martin. The fact she thought he was a loser. The fact he agreed with her. He was tired of feeling the way he felt, and there was only one person he could count on right now. He picked up his phone and looked for the last number he dialed and pressed send. As the phone rang, the familiar voice on the other end picked up.

"Hello."

"I'm coming over."

"What... now?"

"Yes, now. I'll be there in fifteen minutes."

"Well, okay."

He hung up the phone. It was that easy with Elaine. All he had to say was 'I'm coming over' and there was nothing else to the conversation. All he had to do was speak and she responded. He liked that most about her. There was never any pushback. As he drove, he thought about the contrast between his two lovers. Physically, they couldn't be further apart. Elaine was a pale, five-foot-seven, redhead with deep blue eyes. Although he often thought she dyed her hair since he roots were darker than the rest of her hair, he still liked it. Her ginger hair matched her fiery personality. She was always fit, since she was still technically enlisted and had to do p.t. daily. Her breasts were fake, but proportional, and overall, she was well put together. Kendra, on the other hand, was a dark-skinned, beautiful, girl-next-door type who stood only five-foot-four. She wasn't as fit as Elaine, but she did work at it. Much softer since she didn't mind eating a bag of chips or catfish nuggets, but a very curvy physique that turned him on. Intellectually, they weren't very far apart. Elaine was smart, but she could be over-impressed with herself at times, mainly because she went back to school after the war and got her degree, a fact she brought up at any given opportunity. Kendra was smart and confident in her own abilities when it came to work. She had a general knowledge of just about everything, but at the cost of coming off as arrogant, especially when work was the topic of conversation. Emotionally, he knew Kendra was just a tough exterior because she was so soft on the inside. He didn't know much about Elaine's emotions. He hadn't really bothered to find out. He knew she was passionate in the bedroom, and that had to count for something.

He thought about his "Pre-Cal Ken" comment as he parked his truck. He knew it hurt her. After all, that's why he said it. He wanted to hurt her. But he figured she wouldn't return fire as hard as she did. He couldn't shake the fact she thought he was a loser, or he couldn't take care of himself. He wanted revenge for that. He was certain that his Pre-Cal Ken comment, even though it was low, wouldn't hurt her as much as what he was about to do now. He got out of his Toyota and walked into the apartment complex where Elaine lived. It was a new complex, made of gray sandstone cut in large rectangular blocks. It was built to give military personnel who didn't live on base a quick commute to work. Before he bought his house, he thought he would live here for the military discount, but decided against staying so close. He wanted to leave the military behind, and knew dealing with Elaine was a step in the wrong direction.

"Sarge?"

A familiar voice echoed behind him. He turned to see a short, Hispanic male with a buzz cut who used to be under his command.

"Rodriguez?"

"Oh, shit, it's Sergeant Winters!" the young man exclaimed as he walked over to give Marcus a bear hug. One the former Sergeant Winters returned with equal energy.

"Saul Rodriguez! How are you, man?!"

"Doing good, Sarge! Man, it's great to see you. What are you doing out here?"

"Coming to see a friend."

"Who, Jackson?"

"No... Corporal Holt."

The young man nodded. Marcus could tell the guy was suspicious about the time of night, but he still wanted to believe in him, his former sergeant. So, Marcus began to lie.

"Yeah, one of the guys from B Company is having flashbacks, but he'll only talk to me. I'm no counselor, so I'm not sure what to really say to the dude, you know?" The young man's face lit up as if he still believed in Santa Claus.

"Sarge, you're always looking out for us! You're not even enlisted anymore and going out of the way to check on us."

"No man left behind, right?"

"Right! Hey, how's your lady... what was her name... Ke-ke?"

"Kendra."

"Right. You two still good?"

"Better than ever. She's the one that told me to come talk to Holt."

"Oh, that's sweet. You guys are like a power couple."

Marcus rolled his eyes. It was a sentiment Kendra often used. In fact, she used it so often that he despised it. *Power couple, my ass,* he thought to himself, wondering where his power had gone. Rodriguez continued his interrogation.

"What are you doing these days?"

"I... I'm starting a business."

"Oh, cool! What kind of company?"

"It's um... it... has to do with oil and gas."

"Cool. What's the name of the—f"

"Just drop it, Rodriguez," he said in frustration, a point his young friend picked up on as disappointment crept over his face. He just found out there is no Santa Claus.

Marcus decided to apologize.

"I'm sorry, man. That came out wrong. It's just I want to keep it under wraps, you know? It's already taken a lot of energy outta me."

"Oh, man, I get it. No problem. You're a natural leader. I knew you were going to go far in life, and oil and gas? That's where the big bucks are, Sarge. Hopefully, when I get out the service, you'll remember me and maybe give me a job, eh?"

"Yeah, there's still a lot to do, but we're getting there. Right now, I'm just concerned about this soldier."

"No, I get that totally. Did you know that Hayes tried to eat his own gun?"

The words forced a visceral, anguished reaction out of Marcus.

"No... I didn't know that."

"Yeah, it was pretty messed up. I don't know if it was a gun. Maybe he tried to cut his wrist. But either way, I know he tried to end it all. I think Holt is counseling him, but I'm sure he'd love hearing from you. Maybe you could do for him what you're doing for this other guy."

"No doubt."

Marcus shook his head in dismay about the news of another soldier hurting. That man's life was more important than all the lies he told, and the guilt was creeping in.

"Hey, Sarge, I never did properly get to thank you. We were pinned down and under suppression fire. I don't mind telling you I was scared shitless. We all thought we were going to die, but you pulled us together and chewed our asses out. I'll never forget what you said: 'I know you think it's bad now, but I don't give a shit. We're getting out of here 'cause that's an order, and you're gonna execute my goddamn order! You wanna know why? Because you are Bravo Company! And Bravo doesn't quit! Bravo doesn't surrender! Bravo doesn't fail! Bravo fights!' You were so confident, and I believed you. Hell, we all believed in you, and that got us out of there—all of us—in once piece. Thank you for saving our lives, man."

Marcus fought back the urge to choke up.

"It was my job to bring you back home, soldier."

The young soldier stuck his chest out and began to scream, "Because you are Bravo Company! And Bravo doesn't quit! Bravo doesn't surrender! Bravo doesn't fail! Bravo fights!" The two gave one final embrace, and Marcus at last walked away, though his set of emotions shifted heavily. He had been upset with Kendra, but now he was more upset with himself.

"Fuck, I am a loser!" he said aloud. He wanted a drink, and he wanted to vent. He wondered what Elaine had in the liquor cabinet.

As he knocked on her door, the voice on the other end shouted, "That took a lot longer than fifteen minutes!"

"Open the god damn door, Elaine!" he barked. The door swiftly opened. Elaine was in a black, sheer, satin nightgown, one that accented her fake breasts. Normally, Marcus would be totally engaged, but after his last two conversations, he wasn't in the mood. He stayed stone-faced, unable to show any interest in her.

"Like, what the hell?" she yelled at him as he barged past her. He could tell she felt disregarded. He played unaware as she closed the door and turned to face him.

"What?"

"That was rude, Marcus."

"What was rude?"

"You barging in like that. You almost ran me over."

"Yeah, well, in life, you're either a rabbit or a lawnmower. If you don't move out the way, you get run over."

"What is your deal?" Do I have to guess, or do you want to tell me, because judging by the time of night, I'm assuming I'm getting the short end of a lover's quarrel." *Smart girl*

He ignored her accurate speculation and continued to attack her.

43

"Everything is the deal, Elaine. You knew I was coming over. Why are you standing in the door like a traffic cop?"

"Okay, clearly this has nothing to do with me, so calm the hell down."

Marcus walked into the kitchen and searched for the Bourbon he kept at her place. He opened the fridge, but couldn't find it.

"I already poured you a glass. It's in the bedroom," Elaine said, tightening the robe that accompanied her nightgown. Marcus stormed into the bedroom and located the glass. He devoured the glass in one sitting and poured another. Elaine walked into the bedroom and sat next to him. She placed her chin on his shoulder and began to rub his back comfortingly. It was the first nice thing to happen to him all evening.

"Rough night?"

"Fucking epic. I ran into Rodriguez outside. You didn't tell me he lived in the building."

"Marcus, half of B Company lives in the building. Besides, I'm not the leasing agent, so I don't keep up-to-date records on who lives here."

"Yeah, well, we had a talk."

"Really? What about?"

"Everything. He wanted to know what I was doing with my life and why I wasn't where I need to be and what happened to my drive."

"I'm sure that wasn't the case."

"No, seriously, he kept prying. He even brought up Kendra, talking about all her accomplishments. I wanted to hit that son of a bitch square in the jaw."

Elaine moved close to him. "Are you talking about Saul Rodriguez?"

"Yeah." Elaine moved to give him space as she confronted his version of events.

"Marcus, the guy practically worships you. We called him Private Puppy Dog the way he'd follow you around just to be noticed."

"So, are you calling me a liar?"

"No, I just don't see him being the type of guy to rag on you, that's all. In fact, I'm almost certain he isn't that type of guy at all. He has

44

something nice to say about everyone, including Morales, and that guy slept with his fiancée."

Marcus took another sip of his liquor and chuckled. "You're right, Rodriguez is a solid guy. He... I... fuck. My life is so screwed right now."

Elaine moved next to him again and rubbed his thigh. Marcus continued to talk.

"It's not him, it's this fight I had with Kendra. She's—"

"Marcus, let me stop you right there."

"Why?"

"Have another drink," she insisted, sliding the bottle toward him a second time when he rejected the offer. But he held firm.

"Elaine, you don't seem interested in anything I'm saying."

"That's because I'm not interested. It's almost midnight, and I have to wake up and go to work tomorrow. But do you give a damn? No. I would be more than happy to talk about this with you in the morning. My office hours are from nine to five."

"I thought you told me your office was always open."

"I lied. Nine to five."

"Then why did you let me in?"

"Because I thought this was a booty call like normal people want at this time of night."

"So, let me get this straight—you let me in for sex?"

"Yes, Marcus, we are fuck buddies. Hello? Why is that so hard to understand? If you read that text right, I said my orifices were always open. And they are. I'll suck, fuck, and lick anything you want me to right now, but if you want to have a therapy session, I'm going to need some sleep. I got three guys dealing with PTSD coming to the office tomorrow, and I have one guy who can't seem to stop using his fiancée as a punching bag. I want to kick his ass myself, but you know the good ol' U.C.M.J."

Marcus sat back and listened to her vent. He recalled what Rodriguez said about one of their old comrades.

"Rodriguez told me that Hayes tried to off himself." Elaine shifted closer to him, moving her hand to his crotch.

"He did."

45

"What happened?"

Elaine took the glass out of his hand, poured herself a shot, and took a sip of his prized Bourbon. She let out a sigh.

"The same thing that happens to all the guys over there, Marcus. Believe it or not, you're much more well-adjusted than most of the guys who went over there. I hear the stories everyday of horror, and it's my full-time job to put them all back together again. Don't get me wrong—I love what I do, and I'm always willing to help, but it never stops. If I can't turn it off—if I have to carry all this with me—I'll snap myself. So, that's why I have office hours. Now, are you going to fuck me, or what?"

She began to climb on top of him, his mind still on everything going on in his life: Kendra, Rodriguez, Hayes. "Stop" he said, a request she ignored as she continued to rub his manhood responding to her touch.

"You don't believe me, do you, babe? You have so much stress. I'm here to suck. fuck, or do whatever you need to do to get rid of it tonight."

"We could talk."

"Anything but that."

She grabbed his fully erect rod, biting her bottom lip as if the anticipation were killing her. Marcus removed his shorts, but before he could get them past his socks, Elaine wrapped her lips around his dick. She moaned as a combination of saliva and pre-cum slipped from the side of her mouth. She came up for air after the first taste and sighed, "You taste so fucking good." Before he could respond, she buried her face between his legs again and grabbed the edge of the bed. He tried to put the glass down on the nightstand, but was overwhelmed by pleasure and ended up dropping it on the floor, spilling the remainder of the liquor in the glass. "Leave it," she said, coming up just long enough to mutter the words before sliding back down his shaft, forcing it into her throat again. The veins in her neck became exposed due to the pressure he was causing inside her mouth.

"Damn, girl, I think you like this more than I do," he said as he leaned back. She came up and looked him in his eyes with a sinister smile as she slowly stroked him.

46

"It's possible. I love sucking dick." Her actions followed her words as she went back down to continue her quest to fit his entire package in her mouth. Each time her lips moved up and down his cock, he became more intense. "Grab my hair. I want you to face-fuck me," she said as she took off her robe, exposing her perky pale breasts with their pink areolas. He wanted to suck them, but her request was literally too hard to turn down. He grabbed her hair and pushed her head down on his rod. She moaned in pleasure as he thrust himself inside her. "Use my mouth like a pussy, Marcus," she mumbled between trusts. He obliged and became rougher, his body tightening as he prepared to explode, a fact Elaine did not miss as she sucked harder.

"Fuck!" he exclaimed as he released his load into her mouth.

"Mmm," she moaned. The timing made his orgasm last even longer. He was overwhelmed by her ability to swallow his entire load. He couldn't believe how much she actually enjoyed it. When it was over, she never moved her lips from him until every drop was gone and he became limp inside her. As he began to lay down, she removed his member from her mouth. "Feel better?" she asked. He nodded with satisfaction as she curled up next to him.

"Good. Therapy starts at 9:00 a.m. tomorrow."

Within seconds, he was fast asleep.

47

CHAPTER 7
BELMOND LA SAMANNA

The plane landed at 3:15 p.m. Eastern Time. Kendra sat nervously, fighting her exhaustion. The cat-and-mouse game of trying to salvage a relationship filled with problems she couldn't pinpoint had been draining her ever since she went to Houston the first time. And as bad as she wanted to go back to Houston, Marcus made her think maybe she should stay in Virginia. She didn't believe for a second that Ronnie was going to leave the firm, but if she even hinted at it, maybe the company wasn't as strong as Milton had professed. Ronnie didn't seem like the type to be terribly concerned about layoffs. In fact, she seemed like the type to recommend them, but her friend was truly full of surprises. In either case, it didn't matter now. She was gone—away from the United States, away from all her problems—basking in a tropical paradise. This was the beginning of a new start for her. Whether Marcus was cheating or not didn't matter, at least for the moment. She was free. This was a long-needed vacation, and she wanted to spend the time alone. As the pilot instructed everyone to have an enjoyable visit, she looked for her overhead bag. First class meant first in line for customs, yet she always moved with haste in case she was stuck behind a family of five. The last time she and Marcus visited the island, they were stuck behind just such a family—the Jacksons. She remembered their name because they all had the same shirt, something to the effect of Team Jackson, and at first she believed them. The kids seemed sweet, and everyone was quiet on the plane, but by time they entered the customs line, the youngest promptly threw a tantrum, the mother seemed flustered, the dad seemed like he wanted a drink, and the teenage son was a typical teenager annoyed by all of them. She also recalled that by time she got through the line, she needed a drink as much as the parents and had firmly decided she was against children.

As the plane landed this time, she felt much more optimistic about her chances of starting her carefree vacation. She exited the plane and made her way hastily to the customs line. This time there would be no hassle as she was determined to be the first in line and had her paperwork filled out properly. She was going to avoid any of the drama that came with waiting in customs. As she approached the line, she noticed the two customs officials chatting with each other. She waited patiently as they finished their conversation. She noticed one of the women making eye contact with her, but continued her conversation as if no one was waiting.

"Ahem." Kendra cleared her throat to get their attention. The girls continued to talk. She looked behind her, a growing mob of people exiting their flights and approaching as if they were zombies in the Apocalypse.

"Ahem." She cleared her throat again. The girls continued to talk. *This is some bullshit,* she thought, frantically scanning the area. She noticed another line open, a lone man waiting to help travelers. She hastily walked over to the line, the ever-growing mob of people gaining on her. *Come on, girl, move it!* The last thing she wanted was to be in a line with a mass of people. She reached the counter, arm outstretched, seconds before the next person in line. The gentleman narrowed his eyes as she presented her passport and pointed at a sign above his head.

"This line is for retuning nationals only, Miss. Please use the appropriate line."

You have got to be fucking kidding me! She thought, looking behind her to find the appropriate customs lines already full.

"Sir, I was already in that line. Can I just—"

"Miss, please use the appropriate line," the man said coldly.

Lazy, rude mother... She walked back to the back of the customs line deflated. She was now one of the zombie horde moving mindlessly to the front. She looked at the two girls who were talking earlier now diligently doing their jobs.

And these fake, soul-plane, TSA-ass bitches! As she glared at the women, a little girl screamed at the top of her lungs. Kendra now glared at the girl. "I don't believe this shit."

It was Team Jackson. The children were older, but the antics were the same. The dad looked as if he'd already taken a drink, the mom looked as if she wanted another drink, and the oldest son was totally despondent as the youngest screamed and whined in line. Kendra desperately looked for her headphones and placed them in her ears. The line was painfully long, and after half an hour, she was finally at the front of the line, where she went to one of the two girls, who now seemed totally professional. After checking her credentials, the woman said the words she was hoping to hear thirty minutes earlier.

"Welcome to Saint Martin. I hope you enjoy yourself."

Kendra rolled her eyes and snatched her passport before proceeding to grab her luggage, which was the only suitcase remaining on the carousel. She walked to the exit, and as the doors opened, she felt the fresh air of the island against her smooth, brown cheeks. She walked out and immediately noticed the Caribbean vibe, the people casually moving in or out of the airport. There was a smell of curry in the air from the local food spot right outside the airport and the traffic of taxis scuttling people to and from the vicinity. Kendra passed a light-skinned elderly man with a thick Caribbean accent standing outside a minivan that served as one of the aforementioned taxis.

"Do you need trans, miss?"

"I'm sorry?"

"Trans. Do you need transportation?" the cab driver repeated. She was able to understand him this time, his English pitch perfect, though his accent was prominent. Just about everyone in the service industry on this island spoke better English than most because their tips relied on it. Kendra was always mindful of that and tipped well if their English was good. *If its English!*

"Yes, I can use a ride," she responded. The cabbie walked over to take her bags and place them inside his van. Kendra climbed in the front and sat down, enjoying Maxi Priest on the radio. *Lol good detail* Although the trip had started rocky, it was slowly becoming the one she envisioned.

"And where are we going today?" *Have you personally been there Norton?*

"I'm heading to the Belmond La Samanna hotel," she responded. She sifted through her purse to make sure she knew where her cash was. The hotel wasn't very far away from the airport. In fact, it was less than fifteen minutes away. It was a perfect amount of time to reset her mind from the nonsense of getting into the country. *Enjoy yourself, girl,* she told herself, realizing that she was truly alone for the first time since leaving the country.

She put her headphones back in and pressed play. The first song that came on was *A Couple of Forevers* by Chrisette Michelle. It was a song that made her think of him.

Me and you are built like armor. Hearing those words made her instantly regret the entire trip. She wanted to call him and talk about everything she wanted to get back to right. She pulled out her cell phone and opened up her "What's App", a way to talk for free while *Did not know this!* she was in the islands. She searched for his contact info and was about to call when she realized the app told her the last time he was online: 1:31 a.m. She then realized she'd never changed her app from when she downloaded it in Houston, so the real time was 2:31 a.m. *Oop!* Pain hit her thinking about what he was probably doing and who he was probably with. The kind of pain she came down here to get away from. Whatever he was doing, it couldn't have been good. She decided that since he hadn't called at all, she was going to at least tell him she made it.

Hey, I made it. Just wanted to let you know - KD

She held the phone, anticipating a response. None came. She knew he read the message due to the double blue check confirmation. Still, there was no answer.

"Miss, we are here," the driver said. Kendra put her phone back in her purse, checking the app one final time for any indication from him before gathering her belongings. Still nothing. It was time to begin her vacation.

The hotel was beautiful. It was located directly on the edge of the island, and you could see the beach from anywhere on the property. It was a bit colorful for her taste, yet it was the best hotel on the island according to Trip Adviser. The clerk at the front desk was a slender, ginger-brown woman with four-inch-long nails who popped her gum obsessively. Kendra instantly wanted to judge the woman, but held back. Instead, she smiled politely as she gave give her the confirmation number to her room.

"I'm sorry, miss, I don't see that reservation."

"Excuse me?"

"There's no reservation under the number you gave me."

Flustered by her time in immigration, she had very little patience and no filter as she responded bitingly. "This is directly from your hotel's system. It's not my number—it's yours."

The clerk typed the numbers again. "Miss, I don't see the number. Are you sure you're at the right hotel?"

"Since I booked the hotel and that confirmation number came from your website, I would say yes."

Kendra's frustration grew as she was long-past ready to have a drink, and this only fueled her desire.

"I'm sorry, miss, bu—"

"Is there a manager around?"

Kendra didn't want to call the manager, but she was ready to get to her room, and clearly the clerk wasn't able to handle this request. The clerk called over the on-duty manager who had just finished shaking hands with a customer. He nodded in Kendra's direction as he spoke to his employee.

"Janet, what seems to be the issue?"

"Mr. Vee, this confirmation number isn't working."

The manager took the paper from his employee and typed it in. The room came up instantly.

"Are you Kendra Daniels?"

"Have been my whole life," she responded, still highly frustrated.

"The suite is good to go. I'm sorry about the inconvenience."

"No problem. Maybe if Janet cut her nails, all of this could've been avoided," she said bitingly. The manager nodded as he looked at his employee, who seemed to shrink away, uncomfortable with the attention. The manager handed Kendra the key and apologized again. He signaled two employees to help her with her bags to the suite.

As she entered the room, her phone went off. She picked up the phone frantically and went into her What's App messages. Marcus had finally responded.

KD, I've been thinking about our last conversation. All of this is getting too heavy maybe you should take this time as a trial separation so we both can think about if this is what we want going forward. I love you but I need some time... to see if I can support myself.- Marcus Thought it could have been Elake on his phone

Their relationship was dying. It hurt to breathe at the mere thought of it all. She wanted to sit in her room and cry. She wanted to respond "kiss my ass Marcus." She wanted to know what woman had taken him from her. But she knew if nothing else, it was over and she had to accept that Marcus was cheating. She didn't want to be like her mother, who was constantly played by men, only to stay by them. Yet, she didn't know any other way to respond to this situation. She wanted to call Ronnie, but Ronni would probably chew her out like she did the last time they talked. "I'm going to get drunk," she said aloud, fighting off the pain of her lover's infidelity.

She took a long, hot shower before going to the local bar on the beach. After laying out several options for the evening, she ultimately decided to wear the Felicity & Coco white and purple summer dress she bought last spring. She liked the way it hugged her body against the wind, and an evening along the beach seemed like it would be windy. As she walked toward a mirror in the suite, she gave herself the once-over. "He wants to turn down all of this? Well, fuck 'im, girl."

After walking back to the lobby, she looked for someone to guide her to the bar, only to find it wasn't necessary. A large sign pointed her directly to the Baie Longue Bar, the largest bar on the property. The closer she got, the louder the music became. *Murder She Wrote* by Chaka Demus & Pliers played in the background, and she, at last, began to unwind. I love the music name drops

The bar itself was as impressive as the hotel, but much less colorful. Every door was just a window with an outer express frame and silver handles. The tile was all sandstone to complement the bamboo-colored loveseats on the balcony and the tweed crème covers on the full-sized couches. It all complemented the turquoise horizon that surrounded the island. As Kendra got to the bar, she sat down and scanned the area. Several couples were on a makeshift dance floor, and the DJ had said the word "Rude boy" at least three times already. *I really need a drink,* she thought, becoming lonely again. She called for the bartender to come over.

"Good evening, miss. Can I get you anything?" the bartender asked.

"Yes, I'd like a patron."

"Chilled?" the bartender asked as she looked at a couple holding hands a few seats away, annoyed by their happiness.

"Quickly," she responded.

The gentleman took the hint and prepared a double. "Dis one on de house." He winked at her. She nodded at his generosity and took the shot without hesitation. It was Ronnie's favorite drink, and the one she promised her she'd have first.

The song ended, and Mad Cobra's *Flex* came on. She wanted to leave as soon as she heard it, and the bartender, good at reading people, came over.

"Miss, would you like another patron?"

"Well, I think I'm going to say yes to—"

"I don't think so." Kendra turned to her left to make eye contact with the person who objected to her would-be request. She wanted to object herself, but was caught off-guard by a handsome, six-foot-three, dark-skinned man with a freshly shaved head. The gentleman continued his assault on her choice of beverage

"Bartender, look at this woman. She's too delicate to be drinking straight tequila. Let's go with something as smooth as her skin, but as strong as her will. Bring the lady a rum punch with lime, and I would like a D'usse on the rocks."

She was stunned by his straightforwardness. The bartender, who appeared used to it, waited on her to confirm the drink.

"Thanks, but I'm okay."

"You ever had a rum punch in Saint Martin?" the gentleman asked.

"No, I can't say I have," she responded, impressed by his persistence. Outside of his distaste for patron, he was kind of like Ronnie that way. Like Marcus used to be.

"Well, trust me, you're not okay until you do." The gentleman nodded again to the bartender, who again made eye contact with Kendra. Finally, she nodded her approval. She was startled by the gentleman's bold approach and wanted to know why he approached her out of all the women in the bar.

"I'm sorry, did I give you the impression I was—"

"Looking for company? No, you didn't, but it looks like you could use some company. And it certainly looks like you could use this rum punch. We're on a beautiful tropical island, and there's only one cloud anywhere around for at least a thousand miles."

Kendra, gathering the inference that everyone could tell she wasn't in the best of moods, nodded, though slightly agitated by the dark-skinned man's bravado.

"And let me guess—you're here to be the sunshine?"

"Not at all. The rum punch is here to be the sunshine. I'm here to be the weatherman. And I guarantee that after two of these, even the grayest cloud has to go away."

She smiled. He was clever, no doubt about it, and he was certainly easy on the eyes. At six-foot-three, with a chocolate complexion and perfect smile, he definitely fit the bill of tall, dark, and handsome by any woman's standard. His white linen shirt and crème pants matched the ambiance as if he were a fixture that came with the bar.

"Rum punch for the woman and cognac neat for the gentleman," the bartender interrupted.

The man raised his glass in the air.

"Cheers," he said as he drank the cognac without waiting for her. He looked back to the bartender. "Another round, my good man." Kendra hadn't yet started her first drink and the second was on its way. She wasn't even fully convinced she should have one drink with this stranger, let alone two.

"Well, you should," he said.

"Excuse me?"

"You should have this drink, and the next one with me, too. That's what you were thinking, right?"

55

"How did you—"

"A beautiful woman alone on an island at a bar when a man shows up. If you wanted to be alone, you would have already shooed me away by now. And if you only want a free drink or two, you'd already finish that one and be waiting on the next one while making trivial conversation. But I'm still here, so you're thinking to yourself, 'Should I have a drink with a complete stranger?' The answer is a resounding yes because you're curious, for one, and second, we both know I was right when I walked up. You need cheering up, and this is already a step in the right direction. In my experience, rum punch is best for whatever you're dealing with."

She was stunned. He was intuitive in a way she hadn't been accustomed to. He was charming and confident, but didn't come off as arrogant. Most importantly, he was right—she was curious. She took a sip of her drink, then glanced at him, wanting to know more about his deductive logic.

"How did you know I was alone?"

The gentleman smiled as he leaned in to whisper the answer.

"Because no man in his right mind would leave a woman as breathtaking as you sitting here this long unattended."

The comment forced her to blush. It was a charm she was unaccustomed to. There was a twinge of guilt for even talking to the man, and then she remembered Marcus's words: 'Think of this time as a trial separation.' *You know what? I'll do just that.* She indulged heavier in the rum punch.

"There it goes. Do you see that?"

"There what goes?" she replied.

"The cloud. It is already dissipating, Miss..." the handsome gentleman remarked, now fishing for a name.

"Kendra. Kendra Daniels. I'm sorry, I didn't catch your name."

"I am Desmond Baptiste. It's a pleasure to meet you."

He extended his hand to greet hers. *Very nice smile,* she thought to herself. *So genuine.*

"So, Kendra, is it work or personal?"

"Is what?"

"The thing you need to get away from. Is it work or personal?"

"What makes you think I'm escaping anything?" she asked defensively.

"In my experience, it's the only reason people take vacations alone." Again, she was impressed by his deductive reasoning.

"Both, actually, but mainly my relationship. I think I just got dumped via text."

"Ouch. That's the worst."

"Well, he called it a trial separation."

"Let me get this straight. He called for a trial separation when he knew you were leaving the country?"

She finished the first drink and picked up the second one, sipping heavily before responding.

"I asked him to come, but he said no. Told me some crap like he needed some time alone. To make things worse, I found a piece of red hair in his clothing."

Desmond's face visibly turned sour as he heard the words.

"Well, that can't be good, but you already know that. Bartender, bring us a couple of those patrons the lady ordered earlier."

"I thought you said patron wasn't a lady-like drink."

"I said no such thing. I said you were too beautiful to be drinking it alone. But you have company now."

He had an answer for everything. It was refreshing. His company was slowly melting her frustrations away. The drinks came, and he continued to talk as the music changed to *Champagne Life* by Ne-Yo. ♡

"That's the jam," she said, moving her head to the beat.

Desmond motioned her to the dance floor. "Dance with me."

"Huh? No... I'm sorry, I can't."

"Why not? You don't know how to dance?"

"It's not that. It's... I'm... I just can't."

"See, that's where you're wrong. You can. We're two beautiful people, and there's a dance floor. You're already bobbing your head, and I'm already moving my feet. So, all you have to do is move your feet in my direction, and I'll bob my head in yours, and we're dancing."

His logic and charm were undeniable, and with her inhibitions rapidly melting away, she was ready to hit the dance floor. Yet, she still put up one final barrier.

57

"No, I really can't."

"If I'm not mistaken, didn't you tell me your mate says you're on a separation? What happens on the dance floor stays on the dance floor."

His smile was hard to resist. She began to move her feet, and for the first time in a long while, was truly carefree. He was an incredible dancer, and as the liquor took effect, so was she. The longer they danced, the closer they got. She could smell his cologne as they moved to the rhythm of *Everyone Falls in Love Sometimes*. By the time *Girls Dem Sugar* came on, the scent of his cologne was on her. Before long, the bartender was saying, "Last call."

"Do you want to get another drink?" he asked

"Patron, Jeffrey!" she yelled at the bartender.

"Patron for the lady, and another D'usse for me," he said, relaying the request to the bartender in a more sober fashion. In fact, she had no idea what his name was. She thought she heard another customer refer to him as Jeffrey, but wasn't sure. *Bitch, you are drrrunnk.* She briefly thought about composing herself for appearance sake, until it occurred to her she was on an island where she knew no one but this handsome man. And she didn't even know him. The drinks came, and they downed them like the ones before. "Are you staying here, Desmond?" she asked as she bit into the lime to finish the tequila she just consumed.

"I'm right over there." He pointed toward her suite.

"Shut the front door! I'm over there! What room are you in?"

"Suite 12E."

"I'm in 14E. That's crazy!"

"Then allow me to walk you home," he said in a most chivalrous tone. She smiled as he extended his arm. *Bitch, you are drrrunnk!* she thought again. After Desmond closed out the tab, the pair walked arm in arm across the sand, down the alternate path to the villas. It was a very romantic walk under the moonlight as the ocean waves crashed in the background, and she had to admit she was enjoying herself with this man. He was the tranquil island breeze personified. The closer they got, the more somber she became. She knew they would be at her suite first, but she also knew she didn't want the night to end. In all honesty, she was turned on by him—his scent, his smile. He was the manifesta- *mother?* tion of seduction. Under normal circumstances, she'd be tempted, but might have had enough willpower to resist him. These weren't normal circumstances, however. Tonight, she was certain she wanted him in her bedroom. As they reached the door to her suite, she wondered if he knew what she was thinking. He had been a mind reader all night, but if he couldn't sense this one, it would all be for naught. *True dat!*

"Kendra, I had a good time. I just wanted to say I'm not expecting—"

She leaned in and placed her full, rouge-colored lips to his, the flavor of oak from his D'usse still lingering on his bottom lip. The kiss continued, his lips the right moisture, fullness, and size for her own. Something contrary to any kiss she'd had before, including her years spent kissing Marcus. Whatever this was, she had already convinced herself it would not end tonight. She pressed harder, introducing her tongue to his. The kiss was nothing short of electric. Their passion built into a flurry of kisses as she removed the strap of her sun dress in the hallway. His lips moved furiously down the side of her neck with deliberate pressure, as if signaling his intent to find her pleasure points. She was gaining moisture below and fighting with the room key card to open her suite.

His seductive lips met her collarbone as he ran his tongue back up the side of her neck. *Open this fucking door!* she thought to herself as she continued to fiddle with the key card. Desmond stopped kissing her neck.

"Here, allow me," he said. It was the third time he'd read her mind tonight, a mystery she'd yet to solve. But she didn't care. All she wanted to do was have him inside her suite, and inevitably, her body. "See? Just patience," he said as he unlocked the door with her key card. "Now, where were we?"

He picked her up in his arms, gabbing her buttocks as his sensual lips reintroduced themselves to her own. He carried her through the doorway. "The bedroom is on the right," she moaned as he kissed her with newfound intimacy. She rubbed his freshly shaved head, realizing that everything was smooth about this man, including the way his skin felt against hers.

Desmond gently laid her on the white comforter. She recalled imagining how soft it would feel when she dropped her things in the room, but she never imagined this was how she would discover her thoughts to be true. "What are you smiling about?" he asked.

"You always seem to know what I'm thinking. How do you do that?"

"I pay attention to you."

It was the final confirmation. It had been so long since she'd had any real attention—genuine attention—and she wanted to embrace that. She laid back on the bed while he kissed her inner thigh. She trembled at the pleasure his lips brought to one of her most sensitive areas. She assisted his hands in lifting her sundress. She wanted to be naked as soon as possible. As she lifted the dress above her head, she felt the heat of his breath fall on her clitoris.

"Oh," she moaned, falling back to the bed. The decision to wear no panties was a good one. His tongue kissed the top of her clit as the last of her anxiety, her stress, and her frustration melted away. She laid back and closed her eyes, imagining his beautiful chocolate lips wrapped around her clit. As if again reading her mind, he followed suit, his shaved head working its way around her thighs, her clitoris hardening in response to the rapid touch of his tongue. Sensation poured over her like a rushing wave. She gripped his smooth scalp with one hand. She didn't want him to stop, and he didn't seem to need to come up for air. His lips and tongue granted her the bliss he had given her neck and collarbone. She was certain his lips belonged between her legs. As he licked her moisture, she moaned with pleasure. Somehow he knew when to speed up and slow down as if he'd been eating her pussy all his life. The tension she'd been carrying was fully released as she came harder than she'd cum in months. She dug her nails into the back of his shoulders. "Oh, God!" she screamed. Her orgasm was explosive, intense, and beautiful, and she tingled with ecstasy, his gift to her.

As she came back down, he slid his index finger inside her and rubbed her walls as if massaging the sensitivity of her orgasm. It was a pleasurable feeling, something she wasn't really expecting since she clearly just came. As he rubbed her walls, her clit—still hard from orgasm—began to lose some of its extreme sensitivity. Desmond promptly placed his lips right back on her. "What are you do—" A moan completed her thoughts. She was overwhelmed with pleasure again as his lips locked back on her clit, this time with more determination than before. "Oh, my God, I can't believe this!" she screamed. She normally needed several moments to recover, but he was making her body defy convention. Somehow, through the magic of his tongue, he made her cum again without breaking stride. This multi-orgasm was indeed what she had been longing for; something she didn't even know was possible, as she came again with equal intensity, but in a fraction of the time. She gasped for air as he climbed on top of her, her body still shaking with ecstasy. _consent_

"May I enter?" he asked with a smile. It was unusual for someone to ask. Then again, it was unusual to have multiple orgasms. She wasn't accustomed to any of it, and so she unquestioningly nodded her approval. He slowly used his fully erect member to part her still-shaking legs. Her moisture was met by his stiffness and girth as he descended halfway into her core.

"God, this feels good," she said with a moan.

But he was silent. He instead gently stroked her again, this time slightly deeper. She was willing to take all of him, but he was still toying with her. His third stroke filled her walls with all of his package as she groaned in bliss. He pulled out, his thick, chocolate dick glistening with her moisture. Moments later, it entered her again. "Oh, God" she screamed as his gentle stroke became more intense. She flattened her back to allow him full access to her. He raised her legs in the air as he continued his masterful stroke, picking up intensity with each thrust. It wasn't long before he moved at a rapid, strong, punishing pace. A pace that made Kendra scream with pleasure. "I'm cum—" Her body finished her statement by releasing the elation being held within her. She came for the third time, and was immensely satisfied. Exhausted, but satisfied.

Sweating and panting, she looked at the clock. It was 4:00 a.m. He had been inside her for more than an hour. _Da Fuk_,

61

Did he cum? she thought to herself. She wasn't sure, but she didn't care. She came more in this one sitting than she had since college. She looked at his eyes as he examined her breasts and her smile. "Is it okay if I stay the night?" he asked, his smile hard to resist.

"I wouldn't have it any other way." She moved underneath his beating chest. His penis was still fully erect, but softening. He didn't cum, but he seemed satisfied. Maybe he sensed she could take no more. She was glad to have someone be attentive to her needs for once. She thought about the day, and how drastic life could change in a few short hours. This morning, she was in another country hoping to stay with a man who no longer cared for her; tonight, she was laying with the most charming man she'd ever met. The trip started off rocky, but the night was what dreams were made of.

CHAPTER 8

THE MORNING AFTER

B*uzz, Buzz.*
  "What is that noise?" she mumbled to herself.
Buzz, Buzz.

Her work alarm—the one she forgot to change when she decided to go on vacation—woke her up. She could taste the residue of rum punch on her tongue. *What in the hell did you do last night, girl?* she thought as fragments of the night before started to flood her brain. Her upper back was sore, and so were her inner thighs. *Okay, so you obviously gave up the kitty.*

She could hear the ocean in the distance as she opened her eyes half hazily, the most important piece of the puzzle coming into focus.

"Hey there." Desmond lay across from her as chocolate and handsome as she remembered.

"Hey yourself," she replied with a girlish grin. *Grumble.* Had she not felt the pain, she would think it was someone else's stomach. This was an awkward moment.

"How was your sleep?" he asked, ignoring the fact that her stomach had entered the conversation.

"It was incredible. Well, the little I got."

He chuckled. His smile made the morning almost as incredible as the night, and seeing him jogged her memory. There was absolutely no question that the night was incredible. It was true she drank more liquor than she intended to, but sweating it out against his firm physique was equally fun. It erased any possibility of a hangover, though it did leave her famished and less fresh than she'd like to be when entertaining the first man she'd been with since Marcus—a fact that was already making her feel insecure.

"I just wanted to let you know that last night was just two consenting adults having a good time. There's nothing to feel any guilt about."

"How do you know if I'm feeling any guilt?"

"I'm a mind reader, remember?" She wanted to move closer to him, but was self-conscious about her nakedness. Still, she had questions.

"No, seriously. Why did you say that? What makes you think I feel guilty?"

"Good people like you, when they finally stand up for themselves or balance the scales for the first time, always feel guilty about looking out for themselves."

How does this man do that? It was as if he were able to read her mind by looking at her.

"Let me not presume too much. You did enjoy yourself last night, right?" Desmond asked.

"Yes... immensely."

"Then don't overthink it. You're on holiday, and part of being on holiday is getting away from life back home. It's the 'what happens' rule."

"The what?"

"The what happens rule. You know, like anytime someone goes to Las Vegas and plans on getting into mischief, they say, 'What happens in Vegas stays in Vegas.' Or, 'What happens on the cruise stays on the cruise.' It's the 'what happens' rule. You're not accountable for anything you do while you're gone."

"That has to be the silliest shit I've ever heard."

"Silly, but true. What happens in Saint Martin stays in Saint Martin. I'm sure your ex is probably using the what happens rule at home."

Desmond was right. Kendra didn't know what Marcus was doing, but she was sure he wasn't sitting at home waiting for her to return. The fact that he didn't come home the night she left confirmed that much. Desmond seemed to have all the answers, and he smelled enticing. *Wait—how in the world does he smell so damn good when we were going at it all night?* She got her answer as she searched the room. A used towel near the chair and a fading mist from the bathroom told her he'd clearly showered before getting back in bed next to her.

"How long have you been up?" she asked.

"Just long enough to take a shower," he responded. That statement only made her feel more insecure about her own state of being.

"Actually, I think I'll take one now." *Grumble.* Her stomach interrupted her again. *Girl, you have got to be kidding.* She smiled, trying to pretend as if the noise didn't occur.

She slid out of bed, taking the sheet with her to cover her body, only slipping out of it once she was she securely in the bathroom and ready to step into the shower. "This is so embarrassing. My stomach is going to run this fine, suave, sexy morsel of a man away. Get it together, girl. Get some damn food!" she said to herself. After a quick shower, Kendra got dressed in the clothing from the night before. It was the most available thing she could find, and she still loved the dress. Although she initially thought to change before eating, her stomach was growling. *To hell with it. It's right here, and I'm hungry.* She wanted to go out for breakfast, and was sure Desmond wouldn't judge her for her choice of outfit. Not after all the compliments he gave her about it all night. As she walked into the living room of the suite, she studied the room she barely noticed the day before. The entire room was furnished with hardwood, espresso oak furniture. There was a sixty-inch flat screen hanging on a slate-gray tile reminiscent of the one Marcus hung in their home. A thought she was about to dwell on when her thoughts were interrupted. She located a shirtless Desmond standing near the window in nothing but his black Ralph Lauren boxers.

"Feel better?" He asked.

"Much. I hope you don't mind, but I threw on the quickest thing I could find because I'm starving. You want to grab a bite to eat real quick?"

on her card

"Actually, I ordered for us while you were in the shower. There were few options, so I just got a little of everything."

Oh, my... damn! Smart, attentive, and packing. I like the sound of this. She blushed, knowing it was obvious she liked him. *I wonder if he heard my stomach growling. Is that why he ordered in?* Her smile disappeared as her insecurities returned.

"Is everything okay?" he asked.

"Oh, yeah, you're fi... I mean, things are fine," she said, trying to brush off his question. *Get it together, girl. You're acting like a dumbass right now. It's not like you haven't already rode this ride. Why are you acting like this?* Pre-Cal Ken, the nervous bookworm, was coming back. She had been haunting her ever since Marcus made a point to bring up her old doppelgänger. She wanted to say something—anything—but couldn't find the words. As she struggled, there was a knock on the door. *Saved by the bell!* Room service had arrived, and with it, her reprieve.

"I'll get it, Kendra. Do you want to eat on the patio?"

"Sure." *Grumble.*

Dear God, this is so embarrassing, she thought as she smiled at him. He said nothing. Just prepared the plates. Desmond did indeed order a bit of everything. There was bacon, eggs, croissants, salmon, strips of beef, hash browns, waffles, and an assortment of fruit. It was more than enough for the two of them to eat. There were also mimosas for them, although Kendra was more interested in having water considering the night of dehydration that had just taken place. Desmond clearly agreed as he poured both of them a nice tall glass. *I wonder if he heard my stomach earlier... so awkward.*

She watched as he rolled the cart outside next to the outdoor hot tub that came with the suite. Kendra sat in the metal seat with a soft crème mesh backing. It was classy for a hotel on the beach. The patio was naturally dark, perfect for the nights, with a design that was also perfect for natural sunlight on a hot day. The idea was to shade the guests, and Kendra hoped to test this patio under both conditions. As Desmond prepared a plate for her, she couldn't help but appreciate him.

"That's enough food. I'm okay."

He smirked and replied, "You don't have to cute eat in front of me."

"What? I'm not cute eating. That's all I want. Really."

"It may be all you want, but I think your stomach disagrees." *Lol*

Lord, kill me now. It was the ultimate embarrassment—he had heard her stomach the whole time. She wasn't sure what to say, but it didn't seem important as Desmond interrupted her thoughts.

"Kendra, we're adults. I've licked, sucked, and kissed every part of your body. Well, almost. Your stomach growling isn't going to be the thing that turns me off from you."

It was precisely what she needed to hear. *Thank God,* she thought. She truly enjoyed spending time with a man so candid, so smooth, and so intriguing. She wanted to know more about him.

"So, Desmond, where are you from?"

"I am out of Louisiana. New Orleans, to be exact."

"The boot? Okay, nice. I've never been."

"You should come. It's cool."

"What do you do for a living?"

He chuckled and took a sip of water before looking into her eyes and finishing a piece of salmon he picked up right before she asked her question.

"Well... I... am an S.M.E. on women's studies, with an emphasis on female libido and pleasure."

"Okay, so you're a subject-matter expert on pleasing women. You know, I had you pegged as a professor. What school? Tulane? I didn't know their women's lib courses were that progressive. For the record, after last night, I'd gladly take that class. Go Green Wave."

"I don't teach at a university."

"I'm sorry, I assumed. Do you work at a hospital? That's a little ambitious for any hospital, but New Orleans does have a growing medical center."

"No, I don't work for a hospital either."

"Hmm... so you're an independent contractor?"

"Sort of. I'm an escort." *Bingo! Fuck Boi*

She instantly froze. *Did he just say escort?* She became visibly disturbed. She wanted to say the right thing, but the right thing had never been Kendra, *Lord, please let me hold my tongue.*

"Kendra, is there a problem?"

"You're a rent boy? I can't believe I let you touch me with that thing," she blurted vehemently.

"You didn't seem so concerned when this 'thing' was bringing you to multiple orgasms last night."

"That's because I had no idea you were a professional. Damn it, Desmond, you're a male whore! Is there a clinic in this hotel? God, I need to get tested right now. I feel like I'm dying!"

"I resent the implication. A—we wore protection, and B—I assure you I'm much more safe than whatever diseases your boyfriend is dragging back to you." WOW! The shade

"How do you know? Is he your coworker?"

"I don't have to sit here and take this. I had a great time, Kendra. it was nice to meet you."

He stood up to leave, heading toward the bedroom to find his clothes from the night before. Something in her made her stand up to follow him.

"Desmond, wait. I'm sorry, all of that came out rude. It's just a shock, that's all. I did have a good time last night, and I was having a good time this morning. I shouldn't judge you for what you do for a living. Please, sit down. I apologize."

He paused, cautiously looking at her. "Please," she said again. He nodded and walked gingerly to the table and sat down. It was certainly time for mimosa's at this point. Kendra poured both of them one and drank hers rapidly—much faster than she did the rum punch from the night before. *Say something nice, Kendra.*

"I'm not going to get a bill for your services last night, am I?" It was the only thing on her mind. *God, what is wrong with you?* her inner voice yelled to herself. Desmond responded with the poise he'd shown all night.

"No, I'm on vacation, Kendra. I had no intention of making you a client last night. We both came down here to get away from our problems at home. I didn't want to judge your issues. I saw a chance to have a good time with a beautiful woman who was in need of a good time, and I took it. I'm sorry if that offended you."

She could tell he was sincere. He'd been sincere since they met, He didn't lie about any of his motives since they'd been together, a change of pace considering what she'd been going through at home. She nodded, and the two continued to eat their meals. She was curious about him now more than before. He was handsome, smart, funny— why would he be doing this for cash? She wanted to know more.

"So how much do you charge your clients?"

I can see you're not going to let this go, so let's have a real discussion about it."

"I'm sorry, it's just a lot to take in."

"I understand. It's not the first time I've had this conversation, so let me answer all your questions now. As far as pricing goes, it's much more complicated than that. I don't get paid for sex. I know that's what you think, but that's really far from the truth. Most of the time, women don't want sex like men do, so it's not like I'm working every night, or every week for that matter. Mostly it's companionship, and when they have business functions, time out with their girlfriends, or a good vibrator session, I'm out of work."

"That actually makes sense." Her apprehensions were eased by this statement. Regardless of what she said, a part of her was concerned he was sleeping with every client. She took another sip of her mimosa, helping her relax further.

"But to answer your question, a session with me is about three thousand dollars."

She spit out her mimosa.

"Three thousand a night? I mean, you're great in bed, but no dick is worth that much money! Unless you're holding back something I didn't see last night."

"Again, it's more than sex, and it's not necessarily one night. It's companionship. But to be clear, I was off-duty, so I did 'hold back' for lack of a better term. And you'd be surprised at the client list I've built over time."

She was curious. Who were these desperate women paying for sex or pleasure or whatever Desmond provided? "How long have you been doing this?"

"A few years. I graduated Georgia Tech with a degree in automotive engineering. Problem is, it was at the height of the economic collapse, and places like Ford were barely holding on let alone hiring. Between student loans, and well... food, it was truly one of the only jobs I could put together."

She sat quietly. She understood all too well the struggles in finding work at that time. She also understood the struggles in paying off student loans. There was certainly more than met the eye with Desmond Baptiste. A would-be automotive engineer turned male escort. The effects money can have on a person were unquestionable. She thought about her own woes during school, and how she had considered working at a strip club as a bartender like her roommate, Alexis, did. She had even gone as far as setting up an interview at Club Diamond. She recalled the day she told Marcus about the interview. It was still early in their relationship, and he told her that Alexis was actually stripping. He and his friends had seen her on stage at the club. It was then he told her he'd start to pay down her student loans. That allowed her to finish school. She missed that Marcus, but he was long gone. Still, the thought made her feel slightly uneasy about the events of last night. *Drink, girl,* she told herself as she picked up the Champagne and decided to just drink it straight.

"Kendra, are you alright?"

"Yeah, just thinking."

"Look, if my profession is a problem, I—"

"No, it's not that. In fact, I actually understand how you could get in that situation. I was just thinking about how good people can get in bad situations. I'm sorry for judging you."

"If you're really sorry—and I mean really sorry—maybe we can get in the hot tub and finish off the bottle." She glanced at the hot tub, the water still tranquil.

"That sounds good."

Despite all she had just heard, she wanted to spend time with him. He was still charming, sexy, and despite all her thoughts to the contrary, she wanted to be close to him at this moment. Desmond got up and stepped into the hot tub with his boxers on. "What are you doing?" Kendra asked.

"Since I don't have a bathing suit, it was either this or nothing."

She smiled.

"Are you going to join me?"

Looking at the man she spent the night with, his muscles rippling against the water, she stood up and slipped out of her sun dress. She removed the black Victoria Secret bra she had on and walked over to the sandstone step of the hot tub. She put one foot in.

"Bring the other bottle," Desmond beckoned.

She turned back to the table and picked up the unopened bottle of Champagne and brought it over to the hot tub. She paused before stepping in and removing her matching panties. This action invited him to remove his now soaking wet boxers. She slowly stepped in the tub, her naked body on full display.

"You have really beautiful breasts," Desmond said.

"Thank you."

"No, really. They sit so perfectly against the crease in your abdomen. That's Egyptian goddess shit right there."

She smiled and sat in the hot tub, handing him the bottle and leaning back as she closed her eyes. "You know, I don't know why it is, but I feel comfortable with you."

"Well, I'm glad that's the case."

"No, it's more than that. I trust you. I don't trust a lot of people, especially now. I feel so vulnerable since the thing with my... my ex, but I'm comfortable with you."

"I'll be honest, Kendra. I haven't wanted to leave your side since I met you." cause yure getting paid by Ronnie, Fuckboi!

"I feel the same way! Is that wrong? Should I feel that way?"

"There's no right or wrong—there's just having a connection and not having one. And there's no question we have one."

His words impacted her. She couldn't agree more. They had a connection; one they were both openly acknowledging. His occupation didn't matter. How he treated her right here and now was all that mattered. And at this moment, she was alive.

GH yu are desperate!

CHAPTER 9
WHY DO YOU LIKE TO FUCK OTHER WOMEN?, PART II

Marcus woke up to the stench of a booze-soaked carpet. The odor, compiled over the last several nights, was evident. *Oh, God.* He walked over to the window in Elaine's apartment and cracked it. The trash hadn't been taken out since he'd been there. Two nights of take-out were fine, but there were limits to how much uncleanliness he could deal with. Elaine was a military woman, so he knew she had to be familiar with organization. Yet, there was barrack life and then there was life in overseas quarters, and there is a certain level of filth everyone becomes accustomed to. Even so, B Company was held to a higher standard—a standard Marcus personally set. A standard Elaine apparently forgot once she got home. While he was out of bed, he removed the sheets, then picked up the bottle of Bourbon. He cleaned the bedroom before cleaning the bathroom. As he straightened up, he scanned the apartment for Elaine. She certainly wasn't in the bedroom, and as he made his way to the kitchen to remove the remainder of the trash, he realized she might not be home at all.

"Yo, Elaine!" he shouted. There was nothing. He continued to clean, assuming she was gone, until he heard a noise. "Elaine?"

The noise came from the back side of the apartment. Marcus

remembered there was a second room in her loft. As he entered the hallway, Elaine appeared out of the second bedroom.

"Marcus? You scared me."

"I was calling for you, woman."

"Oh, sorry. I was in my roommate's bedroom."

"Roommate? I didn't know you had a roommate."

"That's cause she's rarely here. She's on deployment."

"Oh, okay. Well, I was cleaning up this place. You want me to straighten her room up?"

"Oh, no. She's a real bitch about me having company in the first place. She would lose her shit if someone was in her room. She makes a point to make sure I lock it for her. I had to pay some of her online bills yesterday and must have forgotten my journal in there."

"You pay her bills?"

"It's like watering plants, Marcus. Her laptop is set up in there. I just hit send."

"Fair enough."

"So, are you ready to begin your session?"

He looked at her. She was already dressed for the day in a lavender silk gown *top* with a black suede miniskirt. A part of him wanted to take off her clothing right there, but he did want to get some thoughts off his chest.

"Well, I was cleaning up this pig pen of yours."

"Ha, that's funny, Marcus. I've been busy entertaining."

"No argument there, but I don't remember you being this sloppy when you served under me." *not a good match - it will bother you*

"You wouldn't allow it. In my real office, believe me, everyone is still expecting the 'B Company level' of pristine. I spend half my morning cleaning at work because of you, Winters."

"Well, it's a good thing I'm the only person you treat at home. No way someone would want to walk into a therapist's office that looks like this."

"I'm sure all my patients would if they knew they would get a blowjob before and after therapy. Now, we can talk decorum and cleanliness, or we can have our session. Are you ready?"

"Sure, let's do this."

The pair walked back to the couch. Marcus made a detour to the kitchen and washed his hands, still covered with grime from cleaning. He sat in the loveseat he'd become accustomed to after multiple sessions.

Elaine sat across from him, put her hair in a bun, and opened her notebook.

"We're now in session. Tell me about the first woman you slept with after the woman in Houston."

Marcus was about to stand up when Elaine stopped him.

"Looking for liquor? The glass and cup are right next to you. I placed them there on purpose. You can have your drink, but you have to answer this: why do you need the drink?"

Marcus leaned over the metal coffee table and poured a glass of Crown Royal Black.

"Was this a trick?"

"Not in the least—just a pattern I noticed. But you're not answering the question. Why do you need a drink? What about my first question triggered you wanting a drink?"

He thought long and hard. He took a sip of Bourbon, and then remained silent. He took another sip. After his third sip, he finally spoke.

"It makes me feel comfortable."

"Were you not comfortable before?"

"I was, but—"

"Then what changed?"

"You're the therapist, Elaine. You tell me."

"Alright, I will. I think drinking makes you feel like you're not accountable for some of your actions. It numbs the pain of what you're doing, and instead of thinking about what you've done with a clear head, you like to muddy the waters with liquor."

It was exactly how he felt. He wasn't able to put it in those words, but she was right on the money about his rationale.

"Alright. So, if that's true, then what?"

"At some point, if you ever want to get back to who you actually are, you're going to need to see who you've become with clarity. Step one is to think about these events without any alcohol."

It was truly a solid point. He had never been the type to drink early in the morning. In fact, as he thought about it, he didn't have any urge for a drink in his hand until she asked her initial question.

"I have to give you credit. You're good at your job, Elaine."

"That means a lot coming from you, Marcus. Thank you. Now, to my original question—tell me about the woman you had sex with once you got back to Richmond."

Marcus instinctively wanted to sip the glass of Crown, but he refrained.

"She was a girl I met at the gym."

"Was she cute?"

"Yeah, she looked good."

"So, you slept with her because she looked good."

"I mean, it was a factor, but it wasn't the reason. She listened to me, you know, like she heard me out."

"From what I gather, Kendra listens to you."

"She did."

"You were a platoon leader. You had tons of women who had no choice but to listen to you, yet you never slept with any of them."

"Okay."

"So why do you do it, Marcus? Why do you like to fuck other women?" He looked at the glass of Crown Royal Black he'd been sipping from and downed half of it before answering the question. "Okay, Therapist Elaine, to keep it real... because I have the time to. Kendra... she's too busy for me. It's not just because she's got this big-time career, or because I want a whole bunch of pussy. The amount of sex we were having before was fine. I mean, she could've given me a bit more head, but I bet every man says that about his woman. But it wasn't until she started putting everything before us—and I mean everything—the job, the friends, the promotion. It wasn't till then that I wanted anything on the side. It all made me feel like I was just an ornament. *How the fuck you think Trophy wives feel?*

"Okay, now we're getting somewhere. So, when do you think it started? When did she get too busy?"

"If I had to think about it, it was in Houston, no doubt. She got too busy once we got to Houston."

"And when you returned from Houston, was she still as busy?"

"No."

"So why did you keep it up?"

"What do you mean?"

"Well, you just said you were cheating because she was too busy for you in Houston. Once you got back to Richmond, one would assume that she didn't have to keep up at the same pace. Yet, you were still cheating on her. So why did you keep the infidelity going?"

"You have a point. She wasn't as busy when she got back... but I liked the attention at that point."

"So, you're cheating because you don't get enough attention?"

"I wouldn't put it like that, but—"

"You just did put it like that."

"I didn't mean it like that. I—"

"Then how did you mean it?"

"I wanted... I wanted what we had. Fuck, I don't know. I wanted more time, more talking."

She smirked when he said it. He wanted to know why, but felt he would regret asking. Still, he had to know.

"What was that look on your face?"

"What look?"

"That smirk just now. Something you want to share with the class?"

"It's just ironic, you know. You're a war veteran, a guy who has to be gone months, sometimes years, at a time, complaining about not getting enough time? I'm sorry, as a woman that just sounds pathetic." Wow

Marcus hesitated, neither angry nor hurt by her words, just neutral. Her words only confirmed how he was already feeling. He was pathetic, but not for the reasons she mentioned. He was pathetic because he allowed it to deteriorate to this. Still, he couldn't let Elaine get away with her comment.

"Seriously? Women do it all the time. Isn't that the real double standard? Women will carry on emotional affairs for years before it turns into something physical. At first I thought to myself, *Damn, Marcus, you're being a bitch about this.* But then I started to realize I wasn't. Kendra is a good woman, but at some point, doesn't every woman think she's a good woman? And if every woman is a good woman, then who are all these ho's I keep meeting out here? I mean, when have you met a woman that says, 'I'm not a good woman' or 'I'm a ho'? Is being selfish, inconsiderate, and yes, fucking around, only reserved for men? Don't get me wrong—I don't think Kendra would ever fuck around, but mentally, right now, she's not in a relationship. Not with me, at least. She goes to work, stays at work until almost nine, then takes a shower, goes to sleep, and gets up to do it all over again. To make matters more fucked up, come the weekend, she spends every hour catching up on everything she missed out on. If it's not her errands, then it's her shows, her friends, whoever, whatever. I'm a warm body to sleep next to. We're roommates, and I'm tired of that. And if I were a woman detailing everything I just said to you, you wouldn't bat an eye to condemn me for seeking attention outside of my relationship. No one would."

"So, I'm here to fill the void of attention?"

"Let's see, its 9:34 a.m. I thought you were here to be my therapist?"

"Point taken. I apologize. Continue."

"If this too much for you, then let me know."

"No, I'm fine, Marcus. Continue, please."

He watched her as she shifted her body weight in her chair. It didn't take any of his extensive years of military training to tell she was uneasy about their conversation. Still, it felt good to get some of this off his chest. The last person he talked to this openly was Ronnie, who threatened to expose his actions in the end. And she will too if you stop

"Elaine, women cheat all the time, and when you ask them why, their response is usually because I didn't get enough attention. It's not that different for men just because you get in a relationship. Her supposed friend in Houston wanted me and didn't care if it hurt Kendra or not. At the time, I thought she wanted me, but I think she just wanted attention. You came along because my needs weren't being met, but let's not act like I'm not here to fill some of your needs, too. The sex was just part of those needs. There's attention, companionship, and yes, trust. We both want those things, so we find them in each other. It's why you're talking to me right now. The sad part is, she's so damn busy, she wouldn't know if it slapped her in the face. I

77

mean, how long have we been fucking? Months? And in all this time, she might have found her first clue? Hell, the dog from *Blues Clues* has a better track record. I've just stopped caring to hide it. She still doesn't put it together."

"Don't you think if you were busier, this wouldn't bother you?"

"Maybe, but I'm sick of this fucking argument."

"That doesn't really answer the question, though." He took a large gulp of the liquor in front of him and let out a giant sigh.

"Look, I tried to find a job when I was in Houston. I left the military to help Kendra once she was through with school. We were supposed to be a team. Once she got established, it was going to be my turn to get my shit together. I filled out twenty-five applications online every day, and that was before I went out with my resumé in hand all day long. But there isn't a high demand for drone maintenance and inspection in the real world. The military has a lot of made-up jobs; we both know this. So, since I couldn't shoot or bomb people for a paycheck anymore, I thought, *Cool, I'll go back to school on my G.I. Bill and reinvent myself.* But the more she got promoted, the more she required of me. She even wanted me to sell the house—my house—the one we live in. My house! I busted my ass to pay it off while I was in the Army, and she wanted me to give it up like it was nothing. Just to get something really nice in downtown Houston."

"So, that bothered you?"

"Hell, yeah, it bothered me."

"Did you tell her how you felt at the time? About how busy she was? About her friend?"

"I... when we first got to Houston, she did everything she could to be top dog. I'd always been a leader, so I knew how to follow. I played a support role because it was her time. I was fresh out the military, and she's over here killing it. I was glad for her. Then, one day, a woman knocks on my door, half naked in a trench coat. Well, you know the story. Basically, telling me things I'd never heard. How amazing I was; how under-appreciated I was. The same things you tell me. But the thing is, I started to believe it. I didn't want to leave the Army. I liked it, and I was good at what I did, but I loved Kendra. She wanted me to choose, and I chose her. But she was never appreciative of that choice.

And when the time came to return the favor, she didn't choose me she chose her career. I don't even know if she knows how much she's changed since those early days."

"She's fucked up."

"Excuse me?"

"She's more fucked up now than she was when you first got together."

Marcus sat there processing her words, the liquor now taking effect. She had a point, but he knew she was the wrong person to have a point. His mistress, of all people, giving him advice on how to salvage his relationship.

"Yeah, she's that. More fucked up than she used to be, so that's why I cheat."

"So, there isn't a small part of you that's jealous her career is taking off while you're just sitting here trying to piece your life together?"

He sat up, his eyes wide. "Are you kidding? I'm not jealous, at all. I'm glad she's doing well. I'm her biggest cheerleader. She did better in Houston than she's doing here. But I'm sure once she goes back, that will change, too. I'm glad she has this career. When I first met Kendra, she was so unsure of herself. I thought to myself, *Damn, this girl is such a wallflower, and such a nerd.* I hated school. I didn't know shit about chemistry or math. To tell you the truth, I don't even understand why they pay her so much money now to do whatever the hell it is she's doing, but I'm proud of her. I remember back in the day. When she was studying, I'd just grab her laptop and ask her all these questions, flash-card style, you know? I didn't even know what half the shit on those cards meant—I just read it. I thought she was so damn smart, knowing all the answers. Even the ones she didn't know, she would get the second or third time around. I missed so much time with the platoon helping her get her degree. I thought to myself, *Even if we're not together, she deserved that damned diploma.* And when she graduated, nobody was prouder. I felt like we both walked across that stage. I remember how scared she was about getting a job in corporate America. A guy I knew from B Company's wife did her resumé. I paid Rodgers' wife two hundred dollars to put her resumé together, and then spent the next three months sending out resumés for her. I was

79

about to be discharged, so I didn't give a fuck. I just kept emailing them. I mean, maybe I should've been putting in school applications for me, or finding a job for myself, but I believed in Kendra. I still believe in her."

There was silence after his statement. Marcus could tell that Elaine wasn't happy with his words. He didn't want to hurt her, but he also knew he was just using her until he could figure out what to do about Kendra.

"Elaine, are you sure you're okay with this?"

"I'm a professional. You know Kendra isn't the only one who went to school and had to take a ton of tests as well, so, yes, I'm perfectly fine."

"I know that. It's just—"

"Don't worry about me. You're going to say I knew what this was when I signed up for it. Maybe I did. It doesn't matter. I think the job of every sidepiece is therapist."

There wasn't a lot to say. He knew she was lying. He wanted to reassure her that what they had was more meaningful, but then he'd be lying too, and there was enough of that going around. He wanted a moment of clarity, a moment of honesty, in this world he'd created for himself.

"So what about your sex life?" Elaine chimed in, breaking up his thoughts.

"What?"

"Come on, Marcus. How is your sex life with her?"

"You don't want to go there, do you?"

"I'm a therap—"

"Therapist first. I know, I know... " he said, cutting her off. He didn't believe her, yet he took the opportunity to express what was on his mind.

"I'm gonna be real for a second. The thing about having a dick is variety, and that doesn't mean let's fuck other women. Not all the time. And it doesn't mean swinging or threesomes, but it does mean spice it up a bit. You can't go through life with the missionary position."

"And that's what you think she does?"

"It is what she does, at least lately. She hasn't tried to grow since we started having sex, and I'm frustrated by it. To be honest, I'm glad she's gone."

"Well, what if she meets someone out there? What if someone is teaching her all the tricks you've been passive-aggressive about?"

"Hell, she's not that kind of girl." *Until She is lol*

"All women are that kind of girl. We just need the right teacher." *bingo!*

"That might be true, but that goes both ways. The thing about having a pussy is as long as you have one, someone is always going to be willing to fill it. But once they're done, are they going to be willing to stick around, help you build, protect, and love you, or are they moving on to fill another pussy?"

"You sound like the therapist now."

"I'm just being real. You don't need a degree to know that."

"So, if she found someone, you wouldn't have a problem with her sleeping with him?"

"Not the problem she would have if she knew about us. I can't control that, but Kendra isn't that kind of girl. She's too prudish. She's not..."

"Me?"

"Well... a woman like you."

Elaine grabbed her notebook and started jotting notes in it feverishly. Marcus wasn't sure what to say.

"Elaine, are you okay?"

"I'm fine, other than the fact you just called me a whore."

"I didn't do any—"

"Relax, I'm fucking with you, Marcus. It doesn't matter if you call me a whore or not because we both know I am. At least where you're involved. But I do think that's enough counseling for the day. Why don't we go mess up that bed you just made?"

WTH?, Does she ever think of anything else?

CHAPTER 10
GET TO KNOW YOU BETTER

After spending the morning in the hot tub watching the waves crash against the shore, Desmond recommended they get a closer look at the beach before parting ways, an idea Kendra still didn't fully accept. She was alone, after all, on a topical island and had met the man she imagined she would meet here. She thought about telling Ronnie about her romp, but decided against it when she realized Ronnie would inevitably ask, and Kendra would undoubtedly reveal, his occupation. No, what happens in Saint Martin *stays in Saint Martin.*

The beach was beautiful, the water a turquoise blue, clear to a point you could see straight down to the bottom of the ocean floor. It was even more enjoyable since there was a very cool ocean breeze that suppressed most of the heat from the sun. It was magical, like everything over the last eighteen hours. She didn't really know how to tell Desmond she enjoyed his company. She also couldn't imagine taking a trip like this without Marcus, who still hadn't bothered to reach out since his last nonchalant text message.

She missed him, but she also enjoyed the company she was keeping.

"Is everything okay?" Desmond asked. Kendra smiled. He hadn't bothered to button his shirt, and so his bare chest was exposed. *Damn, he's fine.*

"Kendra?" he interrupted again.

"Yes, everything is fine. I just never imagined my trip would start like this."

"Like what? Being with an off-duty male escort, or not being here with your boyfriend?"

Her eyebrows raised as she acknowledged her reality. "Both, honestly. It's one of those things in life. What a difference a day makes. What's worse, is he hasn't even called to check on me. I guess it really is over."

"What's his name?"

"Um... we don't have to talk about that."

The water splashed against her feet as she thought about where Marcus was and what he was doing. She wanted to talk, but she wasn't sure how much she could, or even should, share with Desmond.

"Look, we're together right now, and you're not gonna have a good time unless you clear your mind, so let's talk about it. Tell me his name."

He was right. She was enjoying herself, but she was also hurting. She wasn't in a position to rack up a massive phone bill talking to Ronnie, so this would have to do.

"His name is Marcus. Marcus Winters"

"Okay, and how long have you been dating Marcus?"

"Since college, I guess. About five or six years now."

"Six years. That's a long time."

"Yeah, it went by fast."

"As life tends to do. So how did the two of you meet in the first place?"

"I met him when I was an undergrad going to Hampton."

"Let me guess—he was in the military."

She paused. "How did you—"

"Well, between the VA hospital, the National Cemetery being right around the corner from your campus, and Fort Monroe always having something going on, it's probably harder to find men not in the military than ones who aren't." Acknowledging his truth, she shook her head in agreement.

"I'm impressed."

"And I'm surprised."

"Why?"

"Well, most of the men in the military I've met have common sense. Letting someone as beautiful as you leave the country alone is just terrible judgment." His charm covered her hurt, if only for a brief moment. She smiled at him as the wind pushed his shirt open, exposing his tightly constructed torso. Marcus was a gym rat, but his body couldn't compare to Desmond's. His obliques were defined like something out of an action cartoon. He made her feel better just by being present, and he certainly wasn't hard to look at. She caught herself, and decided to continue the conversation.

"That was nice to say. I don't know. Marcus has always been a Richmond boy. God knows why."

"I take it you don't like Richmond."

"Not in the least. That's a big part of our problem right now. He wants to stay, and I can't leave fast enough."

"What is it about Richmond you don't like?"

"Oh, my God, everything! Do you have any idea what it's like growing up in a place where everything is named after Robert E. Lee? Robert E. Lee High School, Robert E. Lee Memorial Hospital, Robert E. Lee toilet paper. I'm surprised my ass doesn't have Robert E. Lee imprinted on it someplace."

"Who's Robert E. Lee?"

Kendra stumbled for a moment, surprised that Desmond, an educated man from the Deep South, had never heard of him. "The Civil War general who fought to save slavery. Which is my point. Being this dark and growing up in a place where the Confederate flag is a fashion accessory isn't what I want to do with my life."

"Very interesting," he said. They stopped along the beach, and Desmond jogged over to a local hut and bought two beers. As he returned, he handed her one. As he took a sip of his own, he continued. "So, you hate the South, too, I presume?"

"No, I don't dislike the South. I just want to get out of Richmond."

"Well, if you could go anywhere, where would you go?"

"Houston."

She watched as Desmond took another sip of his Carib. She could tell he found the entire conversation amusing as he pressed the issue.

"So, why can't you go?"

"I can go. In fact, I have a job offer right now, but... it's complicated."

"Sip your beer. It will become less complicated, I promise you." She decided to take him up on his advice. As the suds settled along her palate, she continued.

"My first goal was to get the hell out of Richmond. I wanted to leave and never look back. It wasn't until I met Marcus that I even considered staying. When I got a chance to go to Houston, it was the perfect city. Diverse, busy, and most importantly, no god damn Robert E. Lee."

He took another sip of his Carib.

"So, what are you going to do about getting out of Richmond?"

"I could take the job, but it would almost certainly mean my relationship is over."

"Are you going to let that hold you back?"

"I really want the job. It's important to me. But there are issues there, as well."

"Such as?"

"I'd have to go head to head with a good friend of mine. I don't want to do that. She's the only reason I even have my job after the last time I worked in that office."

"You can always find another job in Houston for another company. *exactly* A woman of your skillset should have no problem getting another position."

There was a pause as she digested what he proposed. Her physical reaction to the idea of starting over at another company was harsh. Her stomach churned, and she soon rejected his idea. She had built her career with Burrows Industries and didn't want to start over someplace else.

"I could get another position, but to be perfectly honest, I don't want one."

"Why?"

"It would be the only time I've ever really run from something."

85

"Now that I don't buy."

She was caught off-guard by his response.

"Excuse me?"

"That's just bull. We just spent the better half of the last hour talking about how you want to run away from Virginia. You're down here right now because you're escaping your relationship troubles back home. You're not uncomfortable with running. So, what's the difference between running from a city and cutting your losses at this firm?"

The question cut deep—too deep. She wanted to turn around and walk away right now, but that would further validate his point. She remained quiet as she absorbed the truth in his words.

"I guess you have a point," she said. "Still, I want the job."

"That's fair. I say you do what challenges you."

"Let's change the subject. Are you taking your own advice?"

"What advice is that?" the dark-skinned rogue asked.

"Doing what you love."

He chuckled. "Not in the least."

"Well, why not?"

"A few reasons. I won't deny it—I've become addicted to fast money, and while all money isn't good money, this pays the bills, and I like my time."

"So, what would you like to be doing?"

"I honestly want to get a job as an automotive engineer. I spent all those years in school earning a degree. It seems a shame I haven't even been able to try it to see if I was any good at it, you know?"

She nodded as they continued their stroll.

"So, why don't you?"

"Honestly, I wouldn't know where to begin."

"Do you have a resumé?"

"I haven't needed one."

"Tell you what—when we get back, let's put one together for you. Won't hurt to try."

There was a silence. She could feel him examining her.

"I can't ask you to do that on your vacation."

"Desmond, if there's one thing I can do with little to no thought, it's put a resumé together. An hour tops."

She watched as he became visibly emotional before responding.

"Thanks. You don't know what that means to me. Hell, I hardly know what it means. This is unbelievable. I owe you one."

"Well, I know a way you can repay me."

"Name it."

"Tell me about your clients." He took a sip of his beer and replied.

"What would you like to know?"

She thought hard. She didn't want to sound insulting, but she wanted to know more about his actual world than his dream one.

"You've told me what kind of women hire you, but what is it like? What are they looking for?"

"Interesting question. If I had to categorize them, I'd say a lot of them are successful, controlling, strong women with high drives for achievement. But on the inside, they have some significant insecurities. They're a lot like you, actually."

"And what's that supposed to mean?"

"You're asking for honesty, so I'm giving it to you. You're smart—probably too smart for your own good—which makes it hard for you to be around people who don't push you intellectually. You can't laugh at mind-numbing jokes, or surf Facebook for hours. You like to always be evolving. You don't know it, but you subconsciously judged me for not knowing who Robert E. Lee was—something I actually know, but was curious to see how you'd respond. You like a strict routine, but at the same time, you feel like a prisoner to it. It matters to you a great deal what everyone thinks of you, but deep down, you feel misunderstood. Deep down, you just want to be as expressive as possible and feed the beast inside you that's clawing to get out. And you probably wrap all this emotion up in an expensive corporate suit each day. If I had to guess, something from Neiman Marcus, since that's where your summer dress was from last night. You moderate how loud, angry, happy, and sad you can be with precision because it's all an act and has to be within reason, when deep down you just want to scream with no clothes on until your throat is raw."

Her jaw dropped. Every word he uttered was as accurate as a dart hitting a bullseye. She had just met the man, but he spoke as if he knew her all his life. In one statement, he had unpacked the last ten years of her life. Even more frightening was the fact he clearly knew how to help someone escape this fate. In fact, he was paid to do it.

"Was it too much?" he asked cautiously.

"It... was what I asked for. Thank you." The two continued to walk in silence. She thought about his words. It wasn't long before she had something else to contribute to their conversation.

"Are the women ever the same?"

"No, not in the least. They are transformed. It's like a weight being lifted off their shoulders. And every now and then they get a tune-up. It works for everyone."

The silence ensued. After an even further pause, she finally spoke. "Desmond?"

"Yes."

"I want you to do for me what you do for them."

"I'm sorry?"

"I want you to take me on as your client."

CHAPTER 11
MEN OF HONOR

"Ninety-seven, ninety-eight, ninety-nine, one hundred."

Marcus finished doing the pull-ups he'd been working on for the last half hour. He walked into his bedroom and felt relaxed. It was good to be home and get back into his routine. After several days spending his days and nights with Elaine, he wanted his own space. As he sipped his water, he looked at a picture of him and Kendra, one they took the first day they moved into this house. A part of him missed her, if only a small part. He wanted to call, but his pride wouldn't allow it. As far as he was concerned, her going to Houston was a deal-breaker. He knew it was just a matter of time before Ronnie told her about their affair. He wanted to tell her first, but each time he tried, he thought about how hurt she'd be. More importantly, he needed her. The house was paid for, but the day-to-day bills were outstanding, and without her income he'd be in trouble. As he looked at the picture, he picked up the phone to check on her. But then he realized she also had a phone, and if she wanted to talk, she knew how to use it. He instead got in the shower. Today was a bit more pressing than his normal workout because he really had nothing else to do. That's when he decided to keep his word to Rodriguez and go check on Ryan Hayes.

Since leaving the Army, he'd done the one thing that was taboo for all armed forces members: left his men behind. Although, after hearing about Hayes, a part of him felt obligated to correct that, and now was as good a time as any. After he got out of the shower, he made sure he was freshly groomed. He put on a black Calvin Klein sweater with a pair of blue jeans and solid black, Nike Cortez tennis shoes.

It didn't take him long to get dressed and get on the road. In all honesty, he wasn't very fond of Hayes, but knew going to the VA was a great idea. It would be good to see some of the guys that used to be under his command, as well as his peers. Those who were still around, at least. He also thought about his own circumstances. Maybe it was time to get a counselor with a little more objectivity. Elaine was there to boost his morale, but it was hard to tell if that's all she wanted. Moreover, it would make running into people less awkward if he could separate his sexual escapades from his personal development. He thought about his encounter with Rodriguez. It made him remember his pride. He could get on his feet without sleeping with a woman he was vaguely interested in. By time he got to the VA building, he felt like a new man. The moment he stepped in the administrative building, there were several familiar faces. Sergeant Winters was home.

"Sarge!" He knew that voice all too well. Private Rodriguez ran up to him in fatigues.

"Rodriguez, how's it going, man?"

"Aw, man, I'm doing good. Just a little p.t. How are you?"

"I can't complain. It's almost ten o'clock. They got you doing physical training this late?"

"Yeah, no more four a.m. mornings since you left."

"You guys are getting soft," Marcus joked.

"I can't complain. I used to hate the wake-up calls, and then if we didn't get up, you'd hit us with buckets of ice."

"Oh, man! I totally forgot about that."

"I didn't. I still jump up at four in the morning from time to time."

The two men laughed as they shared the memory. Rodriguez began to move slightly in order to avoid cooling down during his workout.

"So, what brings you up here? You coming to see Hayes?"

"Yeah."

"Cool. The corporal said you'd be here today."

"Excuse me?"

"Corporal Holt. She told me you were going to be here. I wanted to come say hello."

"I'm sorry, did you say Corporal Holt said I was gonna come up here today?"

"Yeah. I just saw her. She said you'd be up here soon."

"Interesting." He had just decided he was going to be here. It was a spur-of-the-moment decision. There was no way Elaine knew he was up here. He wasn't even sure why she mentioned him at all. Since he was not entirely sure what was happening, he decided to just be quiet about the subject. *She knows you better than you know yourself. Predictable*

"Always great to see you, Rodriguez. I need to get over to Hayes."

"I'll walk you to where he's being, well... where he is."

Rodriguez didn't want to say it, but Marcus knew all too well what he meant. Ryan Hayes was being held under suicide watch. He wasn't sure what made him try to take his own life, but he respected the man, and it was time for both of them to start acting like soldiers again. No man left behind. Ryan was clearly not home yet.

There was a short walk down a hallway toward the back of the building. Marcus hated the VA. It was always unreasonably cold, which is why he prepared for his visit by wearing a sweater. Even that didn't keep him warm, and he began developing goosebumps as he walked toward the room. By the time they got to Hayes's room, he was rubbing both his arms to warm himself up. "You cold, Sarge?"

"Damn VA. It's always an icebox in here."

"Now who's gone soft?" Rodriguez fired back. Marcus nodded in agreement.

"Well, anyway, he's in there. Always good to see you, Sarge," Rodriguez said as he pointed toward the door leading to Hayes. Marcus gave Rodriguez one final handshake before parting ways. As he walked into the room, the tall Caucasian man sat in a chair watching TV. He hadn't shaved in a few weeks, leaving his ginger-brown beard full and long. He was unrecognizable from the clean-shaven sergeant he often had to compete against during their respective stints in Afghanistan. A part of him wanted to turn back around, but he'd come this far. A little further wasn't going to hurt. Hayes turned around to see him and quickly grinned from ear to ear.

"Well, I'll be damned. Now, I know I'm in trouble. They brought in G.I. Negro," Hayes said as he walked toward Marcus.

"What did you do? Join a biker gang after you got out the service? You look like an extra on *Sons of Anarchy.*"

"Your mom loves it. She likes to tug on the beard, especially when she's blowin' me."

"My mom doesn't like white meat, Hayes. Yours, on the other hand, loves dark meat all the time. At least that's what LeBron and the Cavs told me."

"And just when in the hell did you meet LeBron and the Cavs?"

"At the black people meetings we have once a month."

The two hugged and laughed a bit. Hayes was a bit more frail than Marcus recalled, but he was still the same Ryan Hayes. It was good to see him. Marcus realized he'd been away far too long.

"So, what's good with you, man? You doing okay?"

"How the fuck do you think I am, Winters? They got me locked up in here. Of course, they won't call it that, but that's what it is. I'd kill for a smoke. Ah, shit. I said the word *kill.* I guess I'll be in this son of a bitch another three weeks because of that. You know, it's funny—a man can go to a whole 'nother country and become the god damn Grim Reaper, and no one bats an eye, but if that same motherfucker comes back home and doesn't take a piss in a timely fashion, all of a sudden he's certifiable. These are your tax dollars at work, Winters."

Marcus nodded, agreeing with the sentiment. He noticed the bandages around Hayes's wrists, though. He realized which method Ryan tried to use to commit suicide. He reached in his back pocket and pulled out a large metallic object.

"You know how it is, Hayes. They have to meet their quotas. The good news is you got friends in low places."

"Oh, shit, now I know this is bad."

"It's not a smoke, but I'm sure you won't mind." He tossed the object to this comrade, who caught it and instantly started smiling.

"Fuck you, Winters! Is this what I think it is?"

"Only the good shit for you, my friend."

Hayes opened the container and took a big whiff of the fragrance.

"Holy shit! Fucking 1929 Macallan! Now this is whiskey, man."

"Well, you gonna stand there holding it like it's your dick, or are you going to take a drink?"

"I'm drinking, asshole. I'm drinking." Hayes took a swig of the whiskey and began to shimmy in place.

"Good fucking call, Winters. Last time we drank this shit together, the MP's had to pull us off of some Navy boys. I can't remember who found a case of that."

"Yeah, me either."

The two men thought long and hard, and after a brief moment, Marcus had the answer.

"Shit, it was Robertson!"

"That's right! Robertson! Most useless fucking soldier there had ever been. We used to give him all the shit jobs. One day, this cunt goes out on a routine patrol and ends up brining in the mother lode. Case of fifty-year-old Macallan, about forty grand a bottle."

"Yeah, after that day, he didn't ever get a shit job again!"

"Yeah, even the captain was in on the drinking. I thought he was gonna take all the liquor and process it, so I hid a few bottles, but he let us keep the whole case. Man, there was so much of that stuff over there. Seemed a shame the damn bad guys were living better than us."

"That's why I didn't feel bad about a few bottles finding their way Stateside." Marcus watched as Hayes took a sip of the whiskey and handed it to him. He took a sip and returned the bottle. It was good to see the man he remembered light up again. He understood being in the dark all too well. He resigned himself to knowing that being here was exactly where he needed to be. It was time to ask what happened.

"So, you gonna tell me what happened, Hayes?"

"I fell on a knife."

"Looks like you fell on two."

"Well, I'm consistent, if nothing else," the veteran said as he took a swig of the whiskey. Marcus walked over to make eye contact with this friend as the soldier began to relax, admiring his newfound gift.

"Shit, man, I don't know what to tell you. You remember how we got paired up? The orders came through that Alpha and Bravo would be working together?"

"Yeah, I remember the day. You in charge of Alpha and me in charge of Bravo. My entire battalion was pissed," Marcus said jokingly.

"No shit, so was mine. Alpha had nothing but combat victories, but B Company... Hell, you guys were legend. No causalities since deployment. All successful engagements, and you executed every job ahead of schedule. Fucking Rambo couldn't hold a candle to you guys. And my smug ass had to make it a competition."

"Hey, that's military life man. We knew it was coming, JV boys love challenging varsity."

"Watch it, asshole."

"I think we both wanted to see what each other was made of," Marcus said as he took the bottle from his friend to have another swig before handing it back to him immediately.

"Yeah, well, we didn't want to be the second-best platoon in the region. We had to be first. Hell, I had to be first. I wasn't gonna let your black ass supplant me, Winters. Just wasn't gonna happen."

"It was the spirit of completion, Hayes. Those were trying times."

He took another sip of the whiskey and handed it back to Marcus.

"Nasty shit we saw down there."

"No doubt," Marcus said as he took another sip. He was watching Hayes. He had certainly changed over the years. The once well put-together soldier was now a barren, beaten man who seemed not to care about anything.

After a brief pause, Hayes looked at him and asked, "You remember Iron Claw? We got that shitty Intel on that operation, and Coms were on the fritz. We had no idea what command said and weren't sure what our orders were. You wanted to play it safe. Wait for Intel to be repeated. Thought there could be a trap laying in wait. I thought you were being a pussy. Well, at least that's what I convinced myself of. Truth be told, I had a point to prove. We were gonna take that enemy outpost by morning. I dispatched Alpha and was out, even though you were the ranking officer by a few months. We were gung ho heading to kick some Afghan ass, only to find out there really was a trap laying in wait and the outpost was a decoy. We got trapped in the middle of that bitch and were pinned down. To make shit even worse, we got flanked by the enemy a few hours into contact. My soldiers were scared shitless, but I still needed them to fight. I took my battalion into that ravine, and we got torn to shreds. All that fire. I panicked. Nine guys killed, four guys injured because of my goddamn ego. You told me not to go out, but I had to prove that Alpha was better than B Company. We both heard the order, and I disobeyed it. You rescued us. You rescued me and what was left of my squad, and you know, after all the shit we went through, you didn't lose a single guy. You could've had me court martialed, but you didn't say a word." Hayes took another swig of the whiskey before he continued.

"I remember thinking, *Damn, I guess B Company really is better than us.* But now I see you were just a better leader. You wouldn't have risked your guys over pride. I should've never made it out of that ravine. My guys should have; not me. I'm here paying for my sins 'cause there are thirteen families I ruined 'cause of my ego."

"You can't think like that, Hayes. We were faced with immeasurable odds. All of us. You did what you thought was right at the time, and I did what I had to do. Fuck, we all did. There's no second-guessing in wartime. Hell, there's no time. We were soldiers; we execute orders."

Marcus grabbed the whiskey and took a nice-sized gulp. The bottle was starting to affect both of them. He finally asked the question he'd been wanting to ask since he got there.

"Is that why you tried to—"

"What? Off myself? Hell, I don't know man. I was pretty wasted. But I can still hear the screams, man." He sipped more of the whiskey, then continued. "Sometimes I go to sleep at night and I'm trapped in that ravine, bodies of my soldiers all around me bleeding from every fucking hole you can imagine, and even a few you can't, and for what? A chance to be an E-6? I'm a fucking asshole, Winters."

"Well, you've always been an asshole, Hayes, but that doesn't mean you should end your life."

"Oh, hell, don't give me that dippity-do-right shit, Winters. What do you know about what I'm going through? You're a god damn war hero. You got a Distinguished Service Medal for saving my ass. You have it all, man. You don't know what it's like to have real problems. To struggle after you get out of the service."

"You still think it's all about you, don't you? You don't think I have my share of struggles? I haven't done shit with my life since I left the military. I got a lady that doesn't respect me, and I haven't been able to get a job in over a year. And everyone, including you, keeps reminding me that I used to be someone. Well, I'm nobody now, Hayes, and I gotta deal with that, like you gotta deal with the fact you're still that same ego-driven son of a bitch. You want to take the easy way out? Fine! When you get out of here, you find a gun and you end it. You're a trained killer, so none of this pussy shit—no one's gonna stop you. But you want to be a leader, a real leader? Then you step up and you live, Hayes. If not for yourself, then for the lives of the men lost under your command. You owe them that much."

well damn

There was a long period of silence. After several minutes, Ryan Hayes spoke.

"So you're banging Holt, huh?" *She's gonna run him or Rodriguez told?*

"What? No. I—"

"Save the shit, Winters. I'm not judging you. She's pretty smokin'."

"I'm not screwing Holt."

"Whatever you say, man." Marcus watched Hayes take another sip of the whiskey as if to savor what was now looking like near-the-end-of-the-bottle times. Hayes offered it back to him, but Marcus declined. He wanted to know more about how Hayes knew about him and Elaine. *Sure*

"No, seriously, why would you think me and Holt are... screwing or whatever?"

"Because A—I'm no goddamn private who thinks military men don't lie, and B—no woman talks about a guy as much as Holt talks about you if that guy isn't getting his dick wet."

The entire conversation made Marcus uneasy. He couldn't believe Holt was running her mouth about their sex life. He wanted to know how much Holt was saying, and who she was saying it to. Still, he had to ignore the statement. He wasn't sure if Ryan was just prying for information.

"Man, I'm still with my girl, and we're happy."

"Like I said, whatever you say, man." Hayes finished the bottle and handed it back to Marcus, who could tell his buddy was feeling toasty. He was glad to be there with him, but it was time to have a talk with Elaine.

"Well, man, I'm sure you gotta go do whatever it is sane people do. Thanks for the booze. I'm about to drop into a coma. That shit and my meds are kicking my ass."

"No problem, Ryan. Just remember what I said."

"Sir, yes, sir!" Hayes responded while saluting before falling backward on his cot. As Marcus headed for the door, he heard his friend's voice.

"Winters."

"Yeah, Ryan?"

"Thanks for saving my life... again."

CHAPTER 12
MR. BAPTISTE

"Push your titties out," Kendra said as she examined herself in the mirror. The closer it got to his arrival, the more she fidgeted with little details. The night was young, but she was planning ahead and preparing for tonight. Much later tonight. She'd never been with a man whose job it was to please a woman. She thought about the fact that Desmond was so suave and already a passionate lover that maybe this was nothing more than expensive sex. Then she thought about his statement, 'Yeah, I was holding back.' It made her wonder: was she just that deprived with Marcus, or was this man so good in bed there were actual levels to his dick game? As she finalized her outfit for the night, she put on her Chanel perfume. She wanted him to remember the night as much as she would. She knew that with that many women, she would have to be something special tonight.

She left her suite and went over to 12E. She nervously knocked on the door.

"It's open," he said. She suddenly became much more apprehensive as she walked through the door. Desmond was in the bedroom in a white, long-sleeve, button-up and concrete-gray slacks. The leather from his black Johnston and Murphy penny loafers fought for supremacy to fill the air over his Creed Aventus cologne.

"Kendra, you look absolutely stunning," the attractive rogue said. He showered her with compliments consistently, yet another thing she was unaccustomed to. "Please, come in. I've prepared you a rum punch, but only one because I want you coherent during the ordeal." *?! Oop!*

Ordeal? I thought we were just fucking. She didn't want to say anything, but it was curious choice of words. Maybe there were levels to his dick game after all. *Lmao*

"Please, come into the room," he said. As she entered, she saw candles flickering in the bedroom and the ocean through his open window, letting in the salty air. The ocean breeze touched her skin in such a delicate way she was able to feel connected with the island. It was as if she had been living there her whole life. "Okay, Kendra, you won't be needing this. Desmond walked behind her and untied her dress. The outfit fell to the ground, leaving her standing there in her crimson thong panties.

"You are an attractive woman," he said. He took a sip of his Bourbon, a cocktail he already made in anticipation for the night. *makes the sex last longer*

"I have the same rule regarding the drinks, if you're wondering," and she was indeed wondering. She was also wondering about the briefcase sitting on the bed. It was an unusual thing to have on a trip, though it made a lot more sense in a second. He opened the case and pulled out two sets of leather handcuffs. *!*

"So you travel with leather handcuffs?"

"I go everywhere with my work. One can never be too prepared." *! Oop!*

Okay, Mr. Freaknasty, she said to herself. It was a curious thing *Lol* indeed, but she was now more excited than before.

"Before we begin, I want you to give me verbal confirmation on everything I'm going to tell you. Is that clear?"

"Um... okay." She instantly became apprehensive again.

"Kendra, we can't explore your boundaries unless you are totally engaged."

"I'm sorry, I've just never done anything like this before."

"It's okay, I understand. I'm going to be as delicate as I can. Now, the main things you need to know are your safe words. Red for stop, yellow for slow down, and if something is in your mouth to the point you can't say either, then I want you to shake your head left and right and say 'nuh uh.' Is that clear?"

What... the... fuck. There were indeed levels to his dick game. She nodded reluctantly.

"I need verbal con—"

"I'm sorry. Yes, I understand," she said, still nervous about the interaction as he inspected her. The more he looked, the more curious she became.

"I need you to straddle this chair." She looked at the metal chair in the middle of the room, walking to it with her jet-black Saint Laurent heels still on. She sat in the chair without question.

"Very good."

He used the cuffs to tie her hands and feet to the chair. In an instant, she was powerless. She tried to move her limbs, but couldn't. She got more aroused by her lack of control. Desmond then went back to the briefcase and pulled out a satin eye mask.

"I'm going to cover your eyes, and then we can begin."

"Okay."

She was nervous now, but in an exciting way. As he slid the mask over her eyes, she began to moisten.

"Kendra," he said in a deep, sensual voice, "tonight I want to know your fantasy. I am no longer Desmond. You will refer to me as Mr. Baptiste."

The voice sounded similar to Desmond's, but much deeper, much more seductive. She wasn't even sure it was his.

"Desmond, is that—"

Pop.

He hit her with a leather strap he had secretly pulled from the briefcase. The pain aroused her, but she wasn't sure what she had done wrong.

"I told you once—you refer to me only as Mr. Baptiste."

"Okay, I'm sorry. I—"

Pop.

He hit her again, this time with a little more force. She started to panic slightly.

"You will only speak when you are spoken to, and you will always answer each question with manners. Is that understood?"

"Understood, but—"

Pop.

"Okay, red, goddammit! Red! Red! Red!"

He removed Kendra's blindfold. She scanned the room and found Desmond to be the only person there.

"Are you okay? Did I hit you too hard?"

"Yes, I'm fine, but you can't just tie a bitch up, blindfold her, change the tone of your voice, start hitting her with shit, and think everything is cool. I watch too much *Law & Order: SVU* for that shit."

LMAO
Dead

He chuckled. "I'm sorry. Yes, it's only me. Can we proceed?"

"How do you do that with your voice?"

"Oh, it's a trade secret. Years of practice. Are you ready to proceed?"

She did like the leather and was, to her surprise, feeling seduced. She wanted to see where this went.

"Okay," she said.

He placed the blindfold back on her eyes. His sultry voice resumed his interrogation.

"Tell me your fantasy."

"I... don't have any."

Pop.

The leather hit her exposed chocolate buttocks as she jumped and moistened even more.

"Everyone has fantasies, Kendra. Yours is about control. Either you want to be in control, or want to lose it. Which one do you prefer?"

Her instincts betrayed her. She wanted to submit to him fully. She was already complying.

"I see. We're going to have to explore this." He took what was undoubtedly a piece of ice and ran it down the arch in her back, which instantly firmed her nipples. She tried to resist him as the cold entered her body, but she enjoyed it too much. She let out a moan.

"So, you like ice?"

"Yes."

Pop.

"Yes... Mr. Baptiste."

She enjoyed the pain and the ice, two things she never experienced in sex before. Her fully firmed nipples pressed against the cold metal chair, which, combined with the aftershocks of the ice on her back, moistened her pussy to the point that she wanted more.

Mr. Baptiste untied her hands and her legs.

"Stand," he said in his authoritative tone.

She rose, only to hear what sounded like scissors cutting off her underwear. She was now fully exposed—and fully aroused.

The thing about women like you is either you want to give or take power." He lifted her in the air, her arms pressed against what she presumed was his bare chest. He was shirtless now. She could feel his skin, the crease in his biceps as he carried her to the bed. Once she lay there, he tied her legs to the bedpost using the leather straps. She wanted him and didn't want to wait and spoke out of turn.

"Desmond, I wan—"

Pop.

"I'm sorry, Mr. Baptiste."

The strap hit her thick, chocolate thighs, and it was exactly what she wanted. It was why she spoke—to feel the pain of the leather strap against her. This wasn't like any sexual encounter she was accustomed to. He rubbed a hand firmly across her clitoris, and then gently slid down her legs into the center of her. "You're not wet enough yet." She was, in fact, very wet. More moist than she'd been in years. She wanted him inside her, but she had no control over when, or if, he would enter her. The idea of not being in control frightened her, but somewhere inside she trusted Desmond. After all, this was his profession, and she did ask for his professional services. So far, it was well worth every penny.

"Kendra, you're going to open your mouth, and I am going to place something inside. Do not bite until I tell you to."

His command made her uncomfortable. She wasn't sure what to expect. Nonetheless, she complied. As she opened her mouth, she felt Desmond lightly place something between her teeth, but she wasn't able to determine what.

"Now bite... gently."

She bit into the object, its flavor unmistakable. He had placed a chocolate-covered cherry between her lips, a treat she loved. How he knew that was beyond her. *note taken*

"They say that chocolate is an aphrodisiac. The same can be said for cherries. It's important for you to know this because I am about to put the remainder of this cherry in your vagina, and I won't stop until I've finished this. Are we clear?" *Jesus Christ: yeast infection pH balance*

"Yes."

Pop.

He hit her with the leather strap across her thighs again. She moaned in ecstasy. Panting, she responded properly. "Yes, Mr. Baptiste."

"Very good. We can begin."

She felt the chocolate enter her, and it immediately began to melt. This was followed by Mr. Baptiste's full lips. He heavily smothered her clit. It was already more attention than she had received in years. He locked his lips around her clit, trapping it firmly in his mouth as his tongue flicked it with increasing speed. She moaned as he continued to suck on her with intent. She wasn't prepared for the sensation, and before she knew it, she was cumming harder and faster than she'd ever cum. She orgasmed in record time. As she came, she felt him finally eat the cherry that remained inside her.

She struggled as she fought to speak. "That... was... incredible. How did... yo—"

Pop.

"I wasn't done with you yet. But I will allow this intrusion because you are new to me."

"I'm sorry, Mr. Baptiste... I...I thought you said you were going to eat the cherry and be done."

"You misunderstood." He removed the blindfold, allowing her to make out his muscular figure in the dark. His lips still glistened from her nectar.

"Look to your right." There was a ball gag on the table accompanied by five more cherries. *- Bitch what??*

103

"I told you I would not stop until I've finished, and as you can see, I am nowhere near finished."

He picked up the ball gag and placed the strap around the back of her head and the ball in her mouth, tightening it until she squirmed, though she couldn't tell if it was from agony or pleasure. She had given control to a stranger, and she was intoxicated by his every action. His dick game had levels. *But there's no dick Tongue Game!*

The dark-skinned rogue then commanded her again. "Now, I understand that you will have a lot of questions, but I have a lot of work to do, so if you want me to stop, you know your safety protocols."

He placed the blindfold back around her eyes. It wasn't long before she felt another of the chocolate-covered cherries inside her, accompanied quickly by his lips. She was overwhelmed by the sensation. He feasted on her in a way she'd never experienced. Her nectar flowed freely over his tongue and lips. She was gushing by the time she reached her third orgasm. He came up for air after the third cherry and removed the gag from her mouth, leaving the blindfold in place. She felt what was clearly a straw protruding from her lips.

"Drink," he commanded. It was perfect timing. Between the sweat and the explosive orgasms, she had lost so much fluid she needed hydration. She drank what seemed like an endless supply of water. She was no longer dehydrated, but she was still breathless, panting and shaking with ecstasy. A part of her wanted him to quit, but the orgasms felt so good, so needed, that she hesitated to say anything.

"Open your mouth," he commanded, and she obeyed. She felt the ball gag go back in her mouth, and eventually felt Mr. Baptiste's lips between her legs. There was no penetration. There was nothing in exchange for this ecstasy—it was just for her. She had never been catered to in this way before. The more she came, the harder he worked, which meant the more sensitive her clitoris became. After what felt like her ninth orgasm, she shook her head furiously.

"Mmhh mhh," she cried out as best she could. The pleasure ceased. She could take no more. He removed the blindfold and the gag and stared deep into her eyes. "Oh... my... God... No more, please. No more, Mr. Baptiste." She begged him because it was all she could do.

She simply couldn't withstand another orgasm. She looked at the nightstand to find one cherry remaining. Desmond picked up the cherry and placed it on her lips, and she quickly ate the entire thing.

"I'm impressed. I didn't think you would last that long." He was talking to the air. Kendra had passed out in the wake of her ecstasy.

God damn Superman!

CHAPTER 13

OPTIONS

Marcus headed to Elaine's house. It was still bothering him that Ryan and Rodriguez were aware of their sexual relationship. He wasn't entirely sure if he was over Kendra, but he was surprised she hadn't called. It had been more than a week since they spoke. Still, he was enjoying his newfound freedom. When he got to the complex, he decided to survey the area. The last thing he wanted was to run into yet another person he had to explain his actions to. *There shouldn't be much activity. Most of the guys should already be at work,* he thought, but then realized it only took one to spot him. Elaine had an off day and it was the perfect time to have a conversation. When he approached the burgundy-colored door of her apartment, he decided to try the handle instead of knocking. Not surprisingly, it was open. *Of course, it's open.* Elaine Holt had all but abandoned any military discipline when she wasn't on duty. As the door creaked open, he scanned the living room.

"Holt?"

There was no answer. He continued his search of the room. It was a mess. A pile of clothes sat in the hallway and dirty dishes were stacked on the coffee table. *Damn, Elaine! Do you ever clean up?*

He walked to the back room, stepping around a throw pillow that sat on the floor. "Elaine?" he shouted again as he moved toward her

[handwritten: what is in there? Have you looked?]

bedroom. He was right near the main hallway when Elaine emerged from her roommate's room, locking the door behind her. She had on nothing but baby blue, lace panties. The contrast of her ocean-water eyes and baby blue panties against her fire red hair turned him on.

"Hey, babe, how did you get in here?"

"You didn't lock the door... and what were you doing in there? Is your roommate back?"

"Oh, yeah, my bad. I forgot. No, she's not back. I was looking for a shirt to borrow. I haven't had a chance to do laundry."

"Is that all you have to say? My bad? You gotta be more careful, Holt. Don't you watch *Law & Order: SVU?*"

"Calm down, Marcus," she said as she walked up to kiss him.

"I'm serious, Holt."

"Okay, okay, I get it. I'll do better," she said nonchalantly "And since when did you start calling me Holt again? Are you reenlisting?"

"No, I don't think so."

"Then no military talk here. Ugh, I hate that name coming from you."

"Apparently, there's no military anything here."

She punched him in the arm. "What's that supposed to mean?"

He rubbed his arm reacting to the blow. "It means you have pretty much abandoned anything we worked on in B Company. The house is always a mess. I know I—" *[handwritten: sounds like a nag]*

"Save the lecture, Sergeant Winters. If you wanted to be in charge of me, you should've stayed enlisted. When I'm on duty, I'm Corporal Holt. When I'm off, I'm Elaine—and that's in all areas, babe. So please, try to remember that, because I hate to clean and I hate when you call me Holt."

"Point taken. I guess it's just being around the guys again. Which is... are you gonna put some clothes on?"

"Why? I'm at home, and you've seen me naked. Is this bothering you?"

It was bothering him. He wanted to forget the conversation and mount her until he came, but he had to make sure the rules were being respected.

"It's not bothering me, but—"

"Do I need to get my glasses?" Elaine walked over to the kitchen counter and put on her reading glasses. She then walked back over to him seductively.

"Tell me, Marcus, when did you first start having these emotions?" she said mockingly.

"I'm not here for your psychobabble, Elaine."

"Oh! Then what are you hear for?" she said as she placed her hand on the outside of his black gym shorts. Marcus pushed her hand away, but he was already strongly considering the same thing.

"You can move my hand, but someone is at half-mast already," she said as she tied her hair up in a bun.

"Holt, we gotta talk."

"About what, babe?" she said in perky fashion.

"Listen, you can't be out here telling people we're in a relationship."

"I didn't tell anyone we're in a relationship."

"Then how did half the staff at the VA know I'd been over here?"

"Maybe because you told Rodriguez you were coming to see me in the middle of the night. And for the record, half the staff is a bit of an exaggeration, don't you think?"

She had a point. He did come up with a terrible excuse when he bumped into Rodriguez. Still, he wanted to make it clear. "Point is, this is an affair, not a real relationship." Oop.

"And what seems to be the difference, in your opinion?" She asked, somewhat defensively. Marcus decided to proceed with caution.

"Look, it's just about keeping personal stuff personal. A lot of times people have unresolved issues. So, discretion is important. It's part of the entire reason to have an affair—to be discreet."

"And so, in a 'real relationship'—your term—you don't have to be discreet. Am I correct?"

"Something like that."

"Well, I have news for you, Marcus. When you come over here and start to fuck my brains out and I'm screaming your name at the top of my lungs against these razor-thin walls, I'm pretty sure my neighbors know who I'm fucking. And since there's nothing discreet about you banging my head against the headboard, it's safe to say they assume we're in a relationship. Should I walk over to their doors and correct them right now?"

"Damn it, Elaine! You know what I mean." The conversation was not going the way he anticipated.

"No, I don't Marcus, but you know what I think? I think you came over here all pent-up because you're dealing with something else, and what you really need is a blowjob." *OIC*

It was a totally unexpected turn in their dialogue. He wasn't sure how to respond. Elaine walked him back toward the crème loveseat in her living room and pushed him down on it. She promptly removed his basketball shorts and boxers.

"Now I know you want to keep arguing this point, but the little big guy here doesn't give a damn, and frankly, neither do I." She began to lick his nine-inch rod from his testicles to its head.

"Now, you can either sit here and discuss the finer points of discretion, or you can sit back while I throat your cock until you cum loud enough to be heard on base. Which would you prefer?"

He remained silent.

"I'll take that as option B."

She went back down on his cock. With each touch of her tongue, his block of frustration melted away. She wrapped her lips around his manhood, first stopping at the head, then going halfway to his base before finally engulfing his entire package. With repeated thrusts from her head into her throat, she pushed his rod into her. She took her hand and massaged his testicles while she deep-throated his cock repeatedly. She wrapped both hands around him as she stroked him, inhaling his rod. The deeper she went, the harder his cock got inside her mouth. She intensified her stroke as he moaned loud enough to *Lol* penetrate those razor-thin walls Elaine referred to earlier. He placed his hand on top of her head and pushed her further down on his dick until her lips were pressed against the top of his testicles. His penis became invisible as she devoured his entire package. The sensation firmed his cock to a climactic buildup. He moaned savagely as he shot cum into the back of her esophagus.

She pulled it out of her mouth and stoked the rest of his load onto her glasses, covering her with semen, his cum dripping from her glasses onto her pale skin, which extended his orgasm for what felt like an eternity. He was finally satisfied, and with his explosion went all his tension. Elaine took the glasses off and licked them. *Bitch what?*

"Somebody's been eating strawberries," she said as he watched her clean her glasses like she was a kid cleaning out a bowl of cake mix. Elaine gave head like she made the concept up. After she finished with her glasses, she licked her lips and sat next to him on the couch, leaning into his slumped-over body.

"I think you're seeing it all wrong," she said.

"What do you mean?"

"It's seasonal, Marcus. You're holding on to history with Kendra, and that was how you were. You're transitioning; trying to build something new and different. She gave you what you needed, and no one's denying that, but maybe it's time for someone else to give you what you need now."

"And I suppose you're that somebody?"

"Who me? No, I mean, I like you and all, but I'm under no illusion about where our relationship begins and ends. Discretion, remember? I just want you to see you're worth more than—Marcus? Oh, my God! Marcus!"

She screamed as he fell to the floor, his body seizing uncontrollably.

I knew there was something wrong with him—arm weakness x2

CHAPTER 14

THE BEACH

"Definitely not the white one," Kendra said to herself in protest. She threw the one-piece swimsuit back into the bag, picked up a purple one—her favorite color—and said, "No, this isn't it either." She threw that one in the same bag. Kendra waited on Desmond to get to her room as she tried on her bathing suits. She still had flashbacks about the last night she spent with him. After her first encounter with Mr. Baptiste, she truly had no idea what to expect. The beach had to be harmless, though. As she put on her teal two-piece bathing suit, she got a phone call from someone whose call she'd been anticipating since she left. She picked up the phone.

"Hello."

"Well, hello, Kendra. Are you having a good time?"

"I have to say yes I am."

"Well, just wanted to make sure you weren't in the hotel room eating your worries away."

"Ronnie, girl, I meant to call you when I landed. I've just been... all over the place."

"And apparently not feeling depressed, which is a good thing. So I take it you're enjoying yourself?"

"Bitch, am I ever! I met Mandingo Brown." *Lol*

"Mandingo Brown. Mr. Magnum, The King of All Pipelayers, you little freak you."

"Stop it, Ronnie."

"Oh, don't tell me to stop. I'm sure you didn't tell him that when your legs were in the air! I need details in 1080P. That's 'P', as in pussy."

Kendra chuckled as she examined her bathing suit. It was too bright against her skin. She decided to go with another color.

"Kendra, focus!" Ronnie demanded.

"Ho, calm down. I'm gonna tell you. His name is Desmond. He was down here on vacation, and we just kind of hit it off. He was—"

"Yeah, that's great. Get to the part where you gave up the kitty."

"Ronnie, you're so damn nasty."

"Again, my man is in a coma. Your sex life is my only form of entertainment." lol

"Since you put it that way, I'll tell you... Okay, so we meet at a club. We're having a few drinks, he's saying all the right things... before you know it, we're dancing until last call. The next thing you know, we're back at my suite getting it, girl."

"Was it good?"

"Girl, was it! We've been sleeping together since I've been here."

"I knew you were a closet ho."

"Ronnie!"

"So, you're done with Marcus?"

"I didn't say that... I'm just going to enjoy this trip."

"So, are you gonna tell him about this indiscretion?"

"We're broken up. There's nothing to tell."

"But are you really broken up? I mean, what if he just needed to blow off some steam and apologizes?"

"I... it happened while we weren't together, so it's moot."

"You think he's going to see it that way? Kendra, come on now."

"Ronnie, are you serious right now? You're the one who told me to meet a guy in the first place."

"I didn't think you'd give it up on the first day!" So day2 would have been better?

Guilt crept into Kendra's psyche when Ronnie said that. She was apprehensive already, but that comment made her uptight.

"Girl, I'm just messing with you. I'm glad your pussy passport got stamped. Lord knows you were overdue." *Dead! Lol*

"Bitch, you had me going for a second. I'm not gonna lie."

"So, when are you seeing him again? And how does he look?"

"Today. In fact, I can't stay too long because I have to meet him, but let's just say if Taye Diggs, Mike Colter, and Morris Chestnut were somehow able to make a baby, and then said baby was raised by Baby-face, and then hit the gym with The Rock, girl, that would be Desmond."

"Damn chocolate deluxe. Well, go ahead, girl, have fun and don't do nothing I wouldn't do."

"So, basically keep my legs open."

"Like a What-a-Burger drive-thru."

"Girl, bye."

She disconnected the call. Ronnie was her usual over-the-top self. *She just got all the need to use on you when you set back* She had a way of pointing out the things that most people didn't want to say. It was always refreshing. Once she got off the phone, she settled on the soft green, two-piece bathing suit and her matching emerald sandals.

"You look fantastic," a voice said, startling her. Desmond was standing in her room.

"What the..."

"The door was wide open. I called your name out a couple of times, but you didn't respond, so I walked in to make sure everything was okay. I hope you don't mind."

"No, I... I don't mind. I'm a little concerned about the door, though."

"I don't know if you closed it the last time I was here. I'm pretty sure a strong breeze could push it open."

The logic made little sense, but she recalled the first day having a hard time with the door as the breeze pushed things around when the patio was open. She then wondered how long he had been in the house. Did he hear any of her conversation with Ronnie?

"Well, thanks for that advice. How long were you standing there?"

"Not long at all. In fact, I just came to bring you one of these."

He presented her with a rum punch. It was starting to climb to the top of her drink list.

"Well, thank you, sir!" she said as she took a sip.

"Are you ready to go?"

"You're timing is perfect. Let's go."

The pair walked out of the hotel room. Kendra made doubly sure the door was closed tight and locked. As they began their journey, the two took the back entrance they used the first night they met and ended up on the beach. By the time they got to the spot where they planned to spend the day, Kendra had finished her drink. Desmond pulled two beach chairs together and settled the cooler with their drinks inside in the sand. Kendra stood looking at the beauty of Saint Martin. It was truly a sight to behold. The greenery, the mountains, and of course, the blue water. There wasn't a cloud in the sky. The beach was heavily occupied, but it didn't seem to matter. She loved the vibe of the island.

"This place is paradise!" she said as she sipped her second rum punch for the day.

"You know the water isn't just for scenery. You can swim in it."

"And spend the rest of this trip dealing with my hair? Black women problems. Helloooo?"

"Why don't you just wash and rinse?"

"See, I'm not going to even entertain that. This is why black men and black women don't get along. You don't understand the struggle for us to look the way we do. I have a natural, but this takes work and... lots of work."

He stood up and walked over to her. "Have you ever stopped to think that maybe we do... understand each other, we just don't care 'cause we like you just the way you are?"

"You say that now, but you would freak out if you ever saw us in our natural state."

"You mean with your stomach growling?" he said, referencing their first morning together.

"Now that is just low, Desmond."

"My point is, you don't have to worry about anyone or anything. I see the natural beauty in you. You're the kind of lady who doesn't ever need makeup because God has kissed your skin. I'm sure he's done the same for your hair."

He gave compliments like he had a never-ending supply. She loved the fact he was so perfect. —until he isnt

"Can I be honest?"

"Of course you can."

"Meeting you has really been the highlight of this trip. Every time you say something like that, you make me see a different me—not the me that has to deal with my real life."

"Who says you ever have to go back?"

"Now you're just fucking with me."

"I'm serious. I'm not saying you don't have to go back to your real life, but you're the master of what that means. Like you don't have to be super smart or super controlling—you can be this version of you."

She kicked the sand with her sandals as she thought about his words.

"Seriously," he said, continuing, "think about what you'd be doing with your life if you didn't have your job and your relationship and your problems. Hypothetically, if you were able to do anything in the world with none of your responsibilities waiting on you, what would you do?"

"I'm not sure. I'd—"

"Come on, Kendra. You are super analytical. Is there an imagination inside that big brain of yours, too?"

She smiled. Being on the beach with this man was carefree, his question intriguing.

"Snow cones."

"Huh?"

"I'd move here... or a place like here and open up a snow cone shop. On the beach for the kids, and then I'd probably make adult snow cones for the grownups. Make a killing and live in a little apartment not too far from a coffee shop. That's my happily ever after."

Desmond smiled and nodded, pleased with her answer. "What about you?" she asked in return.

"Me?"

"Oh, come on now. You can't ask a question like that without giving an answer of your own. If you could get away from everything, where would you go and what would you do?"

Desmond looked into the sky, the sun hitting his deep brown skin and creating a shimmer off his physique. Kendra watched him as he looked to the sky for answers. "Me? Well, I'd stay here, or a place like here, too."

"Okay, and what would you do for a living?"

"I'd make... flavors for snow cones." *stay with you*   *he getting paid*

The answer made her smile. She wasn't sure if he was serious, or if he was just being his charming self. The time they spent together made it hard to decipher what was real and what wasn't. What was this man doing to her? *You're just a customer, Kendra, that's it. This is part of the service.* Still, it was hard to resist his words. They all felt like the texture of honey. Soft, gentle, sweet, and they stuck with you. She was floating on cloud nine.

"Walk with me," he said, rising from his chair and taking her hand. The two headed into the water. The chill from the surf hit her toes and made her want to go back to the beach chairs. But holding his hand, she continued until the water was at her knees. Goosebumps appeared on her body. "Are you cold?" he asked out of genuine concern for her.

"No," she replied. She was, in fact, freezing, but holding his hand was more important than temporary discomfort.

She continued to walk until she was floating, her body acclimating to the water temperature. He turned to her. "I love the water, Kendra —so much freedom." He dipped his head backwards into the water, allowing the saltwater to wash his scalp. He shot his body upright, pushing the waves toward Kendra, who lost balance. She quickly felt his hands wrap around her waist.

"I got you," he said.

His brown eyes shimmered against the sunbeams. She wanted to kiss him, but she wasn't sure if it was out of spite for Marcus, or if she just wanted to kiss him. She placed her hand on his chin as she regained her balance.

"Desmond, I want to thank you."

"For?"

"I don't know how this trip would've turned out if I hadn't met you, but I'm glad I did."

Desmond swam behind her and held her body, at first gently, and then more aggressive. His presence suddenly shifted.

"You shouldn't be thanking him, you should thank me," a deep, sultry voice said. The voice that had given her multiple orgasms since their first encounter. Her body instantly became stimulated at the sound of his voice.

"M... Mr. Baptiste?"

He grabbed her waist tightly, positioning her body next to his.

"I want you to look at the crowd of people," he commanded as he placed his arm loosely around her collarbone, securing her body to his.

"Do you see the children, the parents, the elderly?"

"Yes, Mr. Baptiste." He moved his other hand from her waist to in between her legs. She felt the vibration stimulating her clitoris.

"Wh... wh... what is... what are you doing?" she said, already panting.

"Be quiet, Kendra. I am showing you that the world doesn't pay attention to random acts. For example, the sensation you feel right now—do you like it?"

"Yes... Mr. Baptiste," she panted, finding it hard to concentrate.

"This is a ring vibrator I like to call Mr. Miyagi. It's especially for you. But I need to show you how to use it. You never use him alone. That's what I am for. Next, I need you to look at the people. Do you see them?"

"Yes, Mr. Baptiste."

"There must be dozens of them. I wonder—do you think any of them know you have a vibrator on your pussy right now?"

"No, Mr. Baptiste." She moaned as he spoke in her ear and moved the vibrator firmly over her ever-hardening clitoris.

"So, no one is going to know you're about to have an orgasm in the ocean?"

"N... n... n... no, Mr. Baptiste." She was losing all composure as she reached her peak, the sight of the people totally unaware turning her on more than she could fathom.

"Then cum for me. Cum in front of all these people."

Without hesitation, he pushed the vibrator around her clit. Keeping her eye on the crowed, she released her body's ecstasy, cumming on demand.

Waves of pleasure surged through her body as the ocean waves hit her. She'd just cum in exhilarating fashion in front of countless spectators who were none the wiser. Her body was exhausted from her orgasmic explosion. She had never used a ring bullet vibrator, but now she couldn't imagine life without one. The strength in her legs was completely absent as she floated in the water helplessly. Her hair was about to hit the water when she felt Desmond's arms support her floating frame.

"I told you, I got you." Desmond's voice had returned. It was a statement she'd start to embrace. He had indeed taken care of her every step of the way.

She relaxed as he held her body from the shoulders up, keeping her hair from getting wet. She stretched her neck to kiss him, and he leaned in to accept her lips. The sensation of orgasm was fleeing her body; her strength returning.

"Are you ready to leave? I know you like to sleep after a good 'O'."

She couldn't argue with him. Although her strength was returning, a nap sounded great. Desmond picked her up in the water and walked to the shore.

"Desmond, what are you?"

"Kendra, I... got... you. Just relax," he insisted. As they exited the water, he held her body in his arms. She watched as his hardened chest muscles contracted. *Oh, my. Damn!* Being carried like a princess was too much to deal with. *You are just a customer, girl.* A fact she was rapidly losing sight of.

He carried her toward her suite, Kendra tapped him on his chest while looking back for their missing belongings.

"Desmond, what happened to—"

"Don't worry about it. I took care of everything. I'll explain shortly." He continued to walk toward her suite, a practice that would normally make her feel uncomfortable, but between her rum-punch buzz and the orgasm, her level of concern was greatly diminished. As they arrived at the suite, he placed her feet on the ground. She looked at the handsome, shirtless man in a way she had not done with another person.

"I have a confession to make," he said.

"What is it?"

"Your door was closed earlier. I had the staff here open up the door so a friend of mine could get into your place."

"You did what?" she said anxiously. Her money, credit cards, and passport were in this room. She looked again, and the door was indeed cracked open. In an instant, she went from trusting this man to realizing she was in a foreign country surrounded by strangers. She walked away from him without hesitation and stormed into the suite. As she started to make her way to the bedroom to check on her belongings, she froze. There was a man in the living room holding a knife. Panic set in, but as she turned around to run, she bumped into Desmond.

She turned back around, her senses finally catching up with her fear. She could smell what had to be lobster, garlic, onions, and an assortment of peppers filling the room. She examined the knife-wielding man closer. He was a chef.

"I hope you don't mind, but I took the liberty of having Andre come in and cook for us after our swim. I figured we could stay in, watch the sunset, and eat."

She felt utterly embarrassed. Desmond had once again been a man of his word and taken care of her in every way imaginable.

"This... you... are too much." She had no words for what she was feeling. Desmond no doubt picked up on her emotional tug of war and chimed in.

"Well, I didn't do any of the cooking. Andre is who you should be thanking." She nodded to the burly man who had since put the knife down to work on what appeared to be creamed spinach.

"Why don't you go outside? The cooler with our drinks should be there, along with your personal belongings. I'll come out shortly," Desmond said. She complied, her trust falsely disturbed by her own imagination. She walked outside, poured herself a drink, and sat in the chair. As she looked back, she could see Desmond talking with Andre. Andre, a portly fellow, smiled as he packed up to leave. *How did I not see this big man in my suite when we were walking out?* She realized then that she never bothered to look. She had been too focused on Desmond.

She sipped her punch, chuckling at her ignorance. Or was it her obsession?

"Is it good?" Desmond, still in his swim trunks, asked as he brought the lobster, mashed potatoes with mushroom gravy, and creamed spinach to the table.

"Not nearly as good as what I'm looking at," Kendra said, observing the meal.

"Andre is a beast! We went out on the boat this morning to find this meal. He caught this lobster himself. But he works for the Four Seasons as chef on a neighboring island. He told me he'd hook us up."

"Wait, you did what?"

"We went to get the lobster. That's why I stayed at my place last night."

"What time did you get up?"

"About four-thirty."

She was dismayed. He'd been thinking about her the entire day. It was getting harder to tell if she was just a customer or his lady. Tonight, she decided, there would be no question. She would be his lady.

The meal was amazing. Once she began to eat the lobster, she realized that Andre was indeed welcome anytime he wanted into her suite. It was totally worth being scared half to death. After their meal, Desmond climbed into the hot tub.

"You getting in?" he asked. It was an offer that was hard to resist. Still in her bikini, she decided it was best. She joined him as he stretched his shoulders out, and she placed her head on his chiseled chest.

"So, was the meal worth being a little stunned?"

"I wasn't stunned."

"You were mortified."

"I already told you I watch too much SVU for that shit." The two laughed as they relaxed in the hot tub.

Kendra stood up.

"I have something for you."

She leaned over and picked up her phone. She opened a Word document titled:

Desmond Baptiste - Automotive Engineer.

"What is this?" Desmond asked excitedly.

"It's your resumé. I took the preliminary things we talked about—education, background—and cross-referenced it with what you should've learned and put th—"

"This is incredible. This is truly incredible. When did you do this?"

"While you were hunting for lobster. You're not the only one with skills."

She watched him as he scanned the document. She imagined his face was identical to the one she'd been making since they met.

"Kendra... I... thank you. I don't know—"

"You have done more than I can ever repay. Put your contact information in my phone, and when you're done, send the email to yourself."

Desmond, for the first time, obeyed her command. It gave her great satisfaction to see him as happy as he'd made her this whole time.

They stayed in the hot tub the entire evening, watching the sunset and enjoying each other's company. Mr. Baptiste had already made his appearance, so it was just the two of them. Each day was better than the previous day with this man. A smile reached across her face.

"What are smiling about?" Desmond asked. She wanted to say *I'm smiling about you,* but she didn't want to scare him.

"Kendra?"

"Huh?"

"What are you smiling about?"

"Snow cones," she at last said aloud. Desmond began to smile himself. She stood up and walked toward the edge of the hot tub to look at the now dark ocean and began to scream loudly as if nothing else mattered. She was free and she was happy so nothing else did matter. She screamed until her throat began to hurt from yelling. Desmond applauded her for her expressiveness. She turned back and splashed water in his face with her foot. He laughed as he pulled her back toward her. She stopped her battle cry and moved her body closely to his. He shifted his body from underneath hers to make eye contact, gently kissing her. She returned his gentleness with aggression as she kissed him more intensely. As they kissed, her phone rang. No doubt Ronnie calling for yet *more details*. "Fuck... I'm... let me get rid of this person real quick."

He nodded in agreement. She stepped out of the hot tub and pulled her phone out of her beach bag. In a carefree moment, she picked up the phone and answered it.

"Hey, girl, what's up?"

"Huh?" It certainly wasn't Ronnie on the other end. Her emotions sank as the voice continued.

"What's up, KD. You busy?"

"Marcus?"

"You got a second to talk?"

CHAPTER 15
THE HOSPITAL

"**M**arcus, thanks for checking on me... finally." He could hear the sarcasm in her tone. He wasn't sure why he decided to call her, but now it seemed like a bad idea. His guard instantly went up.

"I figured if you wanted to talk, you'd call. Appears you were busy, so I let you stay busy."

"Don't do that, Marcus."

"Do what, KD?"

"Put it all on me." Her statement annoyed him, and he responded with disdain.

"Isn't all of this on you? Hasn't everything in this relationship been about what you want? That's the thing you don't seem to be getting."

"Marcus, I've tried to get it. You just shut down and shut me out when I try to talk to you."

don't use in arguments

"You know why? 'Cause you don't listen. You never listen, and that shit gets old. You think that you can sustain a relationship with anyone but me? I put up with all kinds of shit from you. I don't have to, but I do."

"This isn't about you putting up with me—this is about you not wanting to go to Houston. Well, I'm sorry. I've worked damn hard to build a career worth something."

"And what's that supposed to mean?"

"Nothing..."

"Oh, I see. What I've done... what I'm doing isn't something?"

"What have you done, Marcus? What have you even tried?"

"I... you know what? It doesn't even matter. We built a life here, KD. Have you even considered... fuck it, you don't even care, do you? It's just you and your career, and it's because of that, Houston is a line in the sand."

"I won't apologize for my success."

"You don't apologize for anything." There was silence on the phone.

"Marcus, can we talk about this when I get back?"

"Why, are you busy?"

"NO... JUST TIRED."

"Well, you know what? Do what suits the great Kendra Daniels. We're all on your time."

"Marcus."

"I gotta go, KD."

"I lov—"

He hung up the phone. He knew what she was going to say, but he didn't care. It was over. Whether out of spite or genuine non-compatibility, it was time to move on. He wanted to tell her he'd been in the hospital for the last twenty-four hours, but the conversation rapidly went from cordial to vicious. Part of his frustration was due to the fact that he had no idea what happened to him at Elaine's house. He wasn't sure what to expect. Elaine had barely left his side since the episode. She'd been a source of humor, insisting he was fine, though she could not stop reminding him how great she was at oral sex. She constantly reminded him that "My head game put you in the hospital." Here he was, fresh off a conversation about denying his relationship with Elaine only to have it totally confirmed in front of everyone he knew. The main thing he wanted at this point was to leave the hospital. He only needed to get the final okay from Dr. Packard, the resident MD who was treating him. He knew the man and trusted his word. Marcus couldn't stop thinking about the irony. In all his time in the military, he'd never had more than a physical checkup at the doctor's office, and now that he was out, he was sitting in a hospital bed. He laughed to himself as Elaine entered the room after finishing her shift.

"Hey, babe."

"Elaine, you don't have to be here."

"Yes, I do. I'm the reason you're here. How are you feeling?"

"I'm doing well."

"Have you had any water today? You have to stay hydrated."

"I know."

"Has Doctor Packard come in to—"

"Not yet, Elaine."

"You don't have to be so dismissive, Marcus. I'm just concerned." She was about to walk off when he held her hand.

"Look, I'm sorry... you're right. I'm not mad at you. It's just a lot to take in."

"I can understand, but you know everything is going to be just fine, right?"

"Yeah, I know. Well, at least I think I know."

"Marcus, you're in great health. You're going to be okay." He turned his head away, not letting go of her hand. After a brief pause, he turned back to make eye contact with her.

"I just got off the phone with Kendra."

He watched Elaine's eyes widen.

"Oh, did you tell her—"

"I couldn't. We started to argue, so there was no time to tell her what was going on."

Elaine squeezed his hand.

"Marcus, I know you probably want her to be here, but you're not alone. I'm here for you."

"I know, and I appreciate it."

"Where is Doctor Packard? I'm going to get a nurse."

"Just relax. He's on his way, baby." Elaine stood up and smiled. Marcus immediately realized what he said and regretted it. He'd never called Elaine a pet name before because he wanted to make sure she wasn't catching feelings—a thing that was becoming close to impossible since she was there for him in his time of crisis. He decided to let it go, considering all that had occurred. Elaine was about to say something when Doctor Packard walked in. His balding head was buried in a clipboard. Marcus observed that the doctor never wore his glasses anywhere but around his neck, and he never made eye contact with anyone—not even Elaine. Marcus assumed he had to be happily married or gay. Elaine made a point to be in attention-grabbing outfits, and they worked on a constant basis. But Dr. Packard only kept his eyes on the clipboard. This time was no exception. In a very nasally voice he talked to Marcus.

"Mr. Winters, we've run just about all the tests we can run. As far as I can tell, you're fine."

"I didn't feel fine on the floor, Doc. Let's be real. Am I going to be okay?" The Doctor examined his clipboard evermore closely, then responded to Marcus's statement.

"Have you been under a lot of stress lately?"

He fidgeted before responding to the question.

"You have no idea," he finally responded. The doctor looked at his chart and then again at Marcus.

"I don't want to rule anything out, but a panic attack has a lot of the symptoms you experienced. There are a few more tests that are going to be done, but for right now I think you're in the clear. I'd like to see you back in a week when we get the results of your blood work."

A wave of relief rushed over him. Considering what some of his former Army buddies were going through, a panic attack sounded wonderful.

"Sweet. So, am I released?"

"You are released for now." The doctor said with a smile. The doctor waved and walked out, again never making eye contact with Elaine. Elaine, excited by the news, kissed Marcus on the lips. It made him slightly uncomfortable, but considering how dedicated she'd been, he ignored his hard and fast rule about discretion. He was alive, and that's all that mattered. Small things like this couldn't stress him anymore.

"Babe, this is great news! We're going to need to celebrate. But no oral, unless you just want to stay in here," she said jokingly.

"Let's just get my stuff and leave," he replied, eager to get out of the hospital.

As Marcus gathered his things, he declined the wheelchair out. He preferred the long walk to the exit to consider everything that happened. The more he thought about it, the more he thought about how Elaine had pushed him with the last blowjob. Maybe what she said all along was right.

"Damn, Elaine, maybe your head is really that good."

"It's a gift and a curse," she said with a touch of mockery.

As they walked down the corridor, the pair crossed paths with Ryan Hayes, who undoubtedly was coming back from another counseling session with another counselor. Marcus instantly felt busted as Hayes made eye contact with him. There was no emotion, but Marcus knew what Hayes was thinking. As they continued to walk toward Elaine's car, he turned around to look to see if Ryan was still staring at him. Sure enough, not only was he looking back, but he was jabbing a finger through a circle formed by his thumb and index finger to indicate he knew Marcus and Elaine were sleeping together. "Fuck my life," he said out loud.

"What did you say, babe?" Elaine asked.

"Nothing. Let's just get in the car."

The pair got inside the vehicle, and Elaine started it up. She then said, "Listen, I know we need to be discreet, but I just really want to kiss you. I'm glad you're okay."

He thought about her offer, and about his conversation with Kendra. He leaned in and landed a kiss on her lips in clear view of Hayes, one that made her blush. She un-parked the car and began to drive.

He was thankful Elaine was there for him, but he missed Kendra. Although he was grateful for Elaine, leaving the hospital made him realize that he wished Kendra was by his side instead.

CHAPTER 16

THE RESTAURANT

"I'm turning this all the way up. Who in the hell does Marcus think he is? Bastard!" Kendra said to herself as she walked over to Desmond's suite. After her conversation with Marcus, she told Desmond to make sure he pushed her as far as she could go. She wanted to forget about ever meeting Marcus. Desmond responded by telling her that tonight was step one. It was the first dinner they'd actually have outside the property with each other. She was excited about the restaurant. So far Desmond had been right about everything they had done. From local beer to horseback riding, she was certainly enjoying herself. A late-night dinner with him was exciting. She decided to go with her La Femme, navy blue, sleeveless sweetheart evening dress. It sat on her body and felt great against her skin. After getting dressed with matching pumps, she walked out of the suite only to be stunned by his presence.

"Hey there."

Desmond stood at the door. He'd chosen a black button-up shirt with slate-gray pants. She could smell the Prada cologne on him, its musk scent watering her appetite for the man.

"Hey," she responded.

"Ready to eat?"

"I am, but listen... about the other night in the hot tub, I just—"

"Kendra, I can't be upset if your boyfriend calls and interrupts us. We're all adults, and I met you with entanglements." — *Is this from Jada days lol*

"You're right. Still, it was rude, and I'm sorry."

"There's nothing to apologize for. From what I heard, you guys needed to clear the air. But we can talk about that another time. For now, let's get to this restaurant."

Kendra nodded. The restaurant was the second time they'd leave the property. This one wasn't very far from the compound, but considering they were both dressed very nicely, Desmond opted to get a driver to drop them off. As they rode in the car, she took in the scenery.

"Where are we going?"

"To a restaurant called Le Tastevin."

"Sounds French."

"It is..."

"That's kind of odd, don't you think?"

"Really? How so?" — *Idiot! what that did colonize af* — *Huh?*

"A French restaurant on a West Indian island? I was expecting to go someplace with a little more curry."

Desmond chuckled.

"Well. Saint Martin is full of surprises. Back when it was colonized, half this island was owned by the French, and the other half by the Dutch. They inevitably decided to just split it down the middle, so places like Le Tastevin aren't uncommon. It also isn't uncommon to hear people speak French or Dutch here." — *this is not his 1st rodeo*

"Once again, I'm impressed. You're a walking Google alert. Thank you for the insight," she said, after which they both laughed.

The restaurant was right off the coast of the beach, like many of the top-tier restaurants on the island. They walked in and Kendra noticed the open floor plan. There wasn't a bad view inside. The sun was almost gone, and a part of her wished they'd gotten here slightly earlier in order to watch it set. She'd been so accustomed to watching the sunrise and sunset with him that she wanted her usual fix. Each one of the restaurants on the island had a slightly varying theme. Most tried to keep white linen tablecloths along with a sandstone tile to blend in with the sand. This one was no different in that regard, yet where they seemed to stand out was their emphasis on customer service. The majority of their staff was young and multicultural, no doubt from one of the universities on the island. As Desmond and Kendra approached the door, the hostess met them. She was a beautiful, ginger-brown local girl with a trained English accent, and accompanied by an equally beautiful, dark-blond-haired girl. Both women were too attractive to be working at this restaurant, or any restaurant in Kendra's opinion. She looked for name tags but saw none. The hostess spoke.

"Hello. My name is Marsee. I am your hostess, and this is Amanda. She shall be your waitress today."

"Nice to meet both of you," Desmond said. Kendra only nodded as she observed the women. Marsee was about Kendra's height and had a darkness to her lips as if she smoked cigarettes on a regular basis, yet her lips looked full of life at the same time.

Amanda was very fit. No more than twenty-four years old, she had a girl-next-door quality, one Kendra saw in herself, which made her glad Amanda was their waitress. She was curious about how the girl got to the island.

"As Marsee said, my name is Amanda, and I will be your waitress today. It's a gorgeous night, and we still have several seats outside. Would—"

"Actually, I'd like to sit inside against that wall over there, if that's okay with you, Amanda," Desmond interjected.

"No problem at all, sir. Right this way."

Kendra was slightly disappointed. She wanted to sit outside and hear the ocean. She wasn't sure why he preferred being inside. It wasn't until they were seated, and he sat next to her instead of across from her that she understood why. He wanted to be as close to her as possible. The more curious part of the night was how Amanda got to Saint Martin. Desmond stated earlier that most of the young foreigners were studying at university, something Kendra disagreed with. She decided to resolve the matter directly.

"Amanda, how did you start to live on the island?"

"Oh, I go to the American University of the Caribbean."

Desmond was once again right. It was almost an easy guess. Many students went here for medical school and to get a great island experience. Amanda asked for their wine selection, from which Kendra promptly requested a bottle of 2010 Wild Horse Cabernet. When the bottle arrived, the waitress explained their specials. She asked if they were ready to eat, but Desmond continued to scan the menu.

"Honestly, I can't find a thing. Can you give us a moment? We'll call you when we're ready."

Amanda nodded and made lasting eye contact with Kendra. It was subtle but noticeable, and certainly didn't go unnoticed by Desmond.

"Well, someone has a fan," he said jokingly.

"What? No, she's just really good at her job."

"I'm sure that's not all she's good at."

Kendra was confused.

"What are you talking about?"

"I'm good at my job, and that wasn't a professional look. Well, at least not in the realm of the food industry."

"Now I know you've lost it," she said half-jokingly.

"Are you telling me you don't find that woman attractive? And I don't mean in a sexual way, but women do acknowledge other women's beauty all the time."

She was slightly uncomfortable with the question.

"She's cool. I mean, she's not my first choice, but yeah, she's not bad looking," Kendra said, hoping to drop the subject.

"Okay, so who would be your first choice?"

"Huh?"

"Female crush."

"I don't follow."

"You just said dear old Amanda there wouldn't be your first choice, so I'm asking who would be."

"My first choice would be a man."

"Oh, don't tell me you ladies do all this lingerie shopping and sleeping over and helping each other pick out outfits, and you never had a girl crush."

"No, that's a male fantasy. Women don't always think with their private parts. Do you have a male crush?"

"Will Smith."

"What? No, come on."

"Hey, I'm honest. I mean, I'm not going out of my way to stalk the guy, but in general terms, he's a good-looking dude."

"Kendra sipped the wine. She looked at the man sitting next to her. His eyes persisted, and she began to entertain his question more seriously.

"Okay, I'll bite. Female crush... let's see. I guess I'd go with a '96 Janet Jackson or current-day Teyana Taylor." *who?. abs!*

"Both excellent choices, in my opinion."

"Possibly Beyoncé... if it didn't break up a home."

"Pre- or post-Blue Ivy?"

"I can't pick an era."

"I'm sure Bey could get it thirty years from now. Have you seen her mother?"

"Tina? Yeah, she'd get it, too."

They both laughed. Desmond leaned over next to her and spoke in a very deep tone.

"Kendra." *annoyed or turned on?*

Her eyes rolled in the back of her head. Desmond was no longer available.

"No, not here. What are yo—"

"Did I ask you to speak?"

"No... Mr. Baptiste."

"Then you must be punished... open your legs."

Kendra looked around the restaurant. Everyone was busy ordering their food or doing their job.

"Don't look at them—open your legs."

She reached her hands underneath the table, lifted her dress, and spread her legs apart.

"This is a beautiful dress. I noticed it when I first laid eyes on you. A friend of yours wants to say hello."

Buzzz. She heard Mr. Miyagi, the ring rabbit. She didn't want to get moist, but she couldn't help but think about the last encounter she had with this vibrator. He placed it on his middle finger like he did on the day they went to the beach. He slowly slipped his hand underneath the table and pressed the vibrator against her clitoris.

not one finger. more control

"Oh!" she moaned.

"You like this?"

"Yes, Mr. Baptiste."

"How does it feel?"

"It feels... wonderful."

"I need more detail, Kendra."

"It feels like you are licking my vagina at a rapid pace."

"And you enjoy this?"

"Yes, Mr. Baptiste."

"What turns you on more? The fact Mr. Miyagi is rubbing against your clit, the fact that we are in public, or the fact that only you and I know that you're going to cum at this table?"

"I..."

He pushed the vibrator onto her clitoris harder. She let out a gasp as the pleasure shot through her body. An inescapable thought breached her mind through the elation she was feeling. She was going to orgasm at this table in front of all these people. It was a forgone conclusion. The only question was could she suppress her moan. Mr. Baptiste whispered in her ear. "You are going to cum, Kendra. I want you to cum, or I'll pick you up and fuck you right on this table until the police get here to stop us." It was all she needed to hear.

"Oh, my God!" The tables near her turned to see the commotion. She didn't care—the orgasm rushed through her system, drowning out any outside noise. Desmond may have taken her to dinner, but Mr. Baptiste made sure she came. Panic set in as she realized she had just *Hot damn* orgasmed in front of a room of strangers. She had no idea how to respond.

"Sweetheart, it's okay. It's just wine—you can get it out." She looked up to see that the bottle of wine they ordered was spilling onto the floor. She never banged the table. Desmond knocked the bottle over purposefully to create a sensible distraction for the crowd. She

was smooth

looked at him, hazily overcome with pleasure as he smiled slyly. The stickiness of her panties, however, was a different issue altogether. She was drunk with ecstasy, having cum in public with no one the wiser. She wanted to compose herself, but she was panting. Through a satisfied gaze, she tried to decipher whether the people at the table truly did not know she had cum. It was hard to tell. She needed to go to the restroom and wipe the fluid trickling down her thighs before it seeped into her dress, but she was still having a hard time catching her breath. "Go ahead and rinse off the wine, honey. I'll get the waitress to take care of this mess."

She complied without a word, but as she slid her way out of the circular booth and toward the bathroom, she heard his voice.

"Damn, would you look at that? I have to clean up, too. I got wine all over me. And here is your purse, sweetheart." She hadn't paid attention to the purse. She was dripping wet and wanted the satisfaction of Mr. Baptiste inside her. Tonight, she wished he wasn't in control. "I'll be out shortly," he said to her as they reached the bathrooms simultaneously.

Kendra walked in, still feeling the aftershocks of the orgasm. She ran the water as she placed her purse next to the marble faucet. When the cool water hit her hands, she received a text message on her iPhone. She wiped her hands to open the phone. It was a picture of Mr. Baptiste, with his pants undone, fully erect in the next room. *Cum play with me.*

Kendra, still not over her previous encounter, almost dropped the phone. She wanted it even before they sat down to order their food, but sex in a restroom in another country? She would die of embarrassment if anyone found out. But his dense chocolate rod was tempting; too tempting to resist. There was no denying her intent as she closed the message. Mr. Baptiste was waiting for her, and before she knew it, she was making her way out of the bathroom and into the next room. She walked out of the women's restroom, surveying the area for anyone who would notice she was moving into the men's restroom. She spotted Amanda, who was on her knees cleaning up the wine spilled at the table. Once again, her eye contact lasted longer than it normally should. Kendra walked into the men's restroom confident the waitress wouldn't say a word.

He was a romantic, a poet, a lover, a friend, and a freak. Someone to be turned on by and disgusted with in the same breath. He filled her with emotion. Whether it was the sensation of an orgasm or the comfort of someone who listen to her, this experience indulged all her pleasurable senses with little to no conflict. It was heaven, it was ecstasy, but it wasn't real.

She took her panties off as she entered the men's room and threw them in the trash. There was only one stall closed and seemingly locked, and that had to be the one he was in, waiting for her. She'd never had sex in a public restroom before, but that was about to change. She walked in and opened the stall. He was there, still looking like the picture he sent her. She kissed him passionately as he lifted her in the air. He placed himself inside her and stroked her with all the passion of the kiss they were exchanging. His force grew as she wrapped her hands around his bald head. Each stroke satisfied her. He moved his lips to her neck where he bit her painfully—a pain she'd come to enjoy. As he bit into her flesh with his teeth on the side of her neck, he let in enough cool air to mix sensations. She panted for life as he entered her repeatedly. The harder he pushed, the harder it became for her to stay silent. It wasn't long before she abandoned all hope of not being heard. He pressed her against the flimsy stall door as he continued to stroke her. He stopped sucking her neck to make eye contact. She could feel him getting harder with each stoke. "Fuck me, Mr. Baptiste!" she moaned as he continued to hit her G-spot, an action which ultimately brought them to simultaneous climax. *no pullout!*

He released her body as she tried to gain her footing. The two cleaned up, opened the stall door, and used the mirror to make sure they looked appropriate. As they returned to the table, they sat down quietly. Kendra noticed the eyes looking at her. There was no question several of the restaurant patrons heard them in the bathroom. *OmG!*

"Whew! I don't know about you, but I am famished. Where is that waitress?" Desmond said aloud. Kendra, uneased by the stares, leaned over to share her apprehensions with the dark-skinned rogue.

"Desmond, don't you think we should leave?"

"Why would we leave when we haven't eaten?"

"People are staring at us." Desmond looked around the restaurant. He smiled and turned back to Kendra.

"So?"

"So, they heard us in the bathroom. Don't you think we should get out of here?"

"We haven't been asked to leave, have we?"

"No, but—"

"So, why would we go anywhere when we haven't had our meal yet?"

She was speechless. He leaned over and kissed her on the lips. He moved his mouth close to her ear.

"Are you embarrassed?"

She thought about his words. She wanted to be embarrassed, but she wasn't.

"No... I'm not."

"You have just had multiple orgasms and are about to have an exquisite meal. You are the sexiest, most beautiful, flat-out most attractive woman in this restaurant. Probably on this entire island, and if I can say so myself, your company isn't too shabby either. If you walk out of here right now, the restaurant will have lost half its appeal. Let's do these people a favor and eat and give them something to aspire to in their own relationships."

His confidence once again tethered on the verge of arrogance, but he was right: one thing no one asked them to do was leave. She reexamined the faces of the patrons in the restaurant. Some of them were smiling as if to indicate they were glad someone was bold enough to get some. Some of them were looking at their spouses in an inadequate way. The more she scanned, the room, the more liberated she felt. It wasn't long before the waitress was back. The woman who was very nice suddenly seemed more reserved and hesitated to make eye contact. This made Kendra even more emboldened.

"Have you decided what you'd like to eat?" Amanda asked.

"I have, but I don't see it on the menu," she said with the bravado of her companion.

"I don't think off-menu items are off-limits, are they, Amanda?" Desmond chimed in.

The waitress blushed and relaxed slightly. "Well, it just depends on what you're looking for."

To which Desmond promptly responded, "I wonder... do you cater?"

CHAPTER 17
WHAT DO YOU WANT?

"Taste this."

"Damn, girl, this is really good."

Marcus was eating what Elaine called a fruit pizza—a cocktail of multiple fruits sitting on a sugar cookie with a spread of crème cheese. He was reluctant to taste it at first. In fact, he was reluctant to have anything Elaine cooked since they always ordered take-out, but in the last few days, she dedicated herself to being his unofficial caretaker, and he couldn't deny her. He sat in the bed watching *Law & Order: SVU* as he finished off the slice.

"You really have a talent for this."

"My mother always told me: You feed a man, you fuck a man, you keep a man." —*But he isnt your man!*

"That's some great advice," Marcus replied. He had finally started getting more comfortable with the time he was spending with Elaine after his incident. The first night he wanted to go home, but Elaine insisted he stay with her, and he didn't put up a fight since she had decided to turn this into an event. Each day, she'd come home and put on a body-hugging nurses outfit with the name tag "Head Nurse". She made a point to cook for him and sleep with him to the point of exhaustion. He barely had to move. Even in bed she did all the work,

Lazy ass MF

stating it was doctor's orders not to stress him out. All things considered, he'd been enjoying the benefits of having a live-in nurse. He enjoyed lying in bed. He felt stress behind his conversation with Kendra. Being waited on hand and foot made him feel important, the way Kendra used to make him feel. A part of him wondered if she had met someone while she was gone, but he couldn't imagine it. She was a workaholic. A part of him thought she never actually left the country. Instead, she just flew down to Houston to start working early. It was totally plausible. In either case, he was certain she couldn't be remotely enjoying herself the way he was. Elaine was pulling out all the stops.

"Babe, after I make this meal, I'll rub your back and take care of you."

He grinned. When Elaine Holt said the words "take care of you," it always meant riding his cock to the point of passing out. He was starting to feel a bit more connected to her in the way people who sleep with each other do.

"Damn, girl, you're really looking out for me. I appreciate it, Elaine." She turned toward him in her skimpy, white latex nurse's outfit.

"Marcus, I care about you. You should know this by now, but if you don't, I guess I'll keep trying to prove it to you."

"You don't have to. I know. I need to act like it a bit more."

The two started kissing, and then Elaine straddled him. It appeared this cock-riding session was going to begin early. As they began to undress, Marcus reached over to the drawer where the protection was. He stopped.

"Where are the condoms?"

"I think we used them all." *not only fucking him! Lol You thought you were special*

"No, we couldn't have. I brought a brand-new pack over the last time I saw you before I went to the hospital, so where are they?"

"Babe, I have no idea where they are. If they aren't in the drawer, then I guess they're gone."

He sat up. Elaine tried to touch him, but he shifted his body and removed her hand from his chest.

"Okay, what's wrong?"

"Why is it we can never find condoms when we're about to have sex?" *She trying to trap you and get prego! or she using them all with many men*

"That's not true."

"I just bought a pack. Where is it?"

"I guess I wasn't paying attention and threw the box out by accident."

"Threw them out, or used them?"

"I don't like what you're implying..."

"I'm not implying anything—I'm being direct. Did you use the condoms I bought with someone else?"

She rolled her eyes in contempt, but he persisted.

"Did you?"

"Oh, God, Marcus, are you serious? When do I have the time? Between work and you living here, when do I have the time?"

"Anytime I'm not with you. Hell, at base, for all I know."

"Unbelievable. You really think that low of me?"

"Not in the least. I just don't like anyone playing with protection like that. It seems like every time we get ready to do something, the protection goes missing."

She rolled her eyes again.

"All that eye rolling isn't a real response. You know that, right?"

"Can I be honest? I hate using those things with you. I want to feel the real you."

"So, are you throwing them out on purpose?"

"No, but I don't feel any remorse if they aren't around. Besides, I'm *until you're* on birth control." She leaned back in, and he shifted again.

"And that's great, but I like life, and more to the point, don't want to have any kids with you." *Oop! Cold blooded!*

"With me... wow, that seems rather personal." He was silent as she withdrew her body from any remaining intimacy. "I see, but you don't mind practicing every chance you get?"

"Never denied that. You're great in bed."

"So, that's all I'll ever be to you?" *She got hooked on that D!*

"Is this a counseling session?"

"No, just a question."

"Elaine, what do you want?"

"I think you know what I want, Marcus. What I've always wanted. We don't have to say it because you know. And what pisses me off the most is that while I would do any and everything to keep you happy, you're still pining after this woman who's halfway around the world doing God knows what with God knows who. Why can't you see that you're better off somewhere else? You think I'm here to be a therapist and a piece of ass for you because I like you? Marcus, I've wanted you since I first met you in B Company. But if what you want is for me to wait in the shadows, fine, I'll wait in the shadows. I'm a soldier first, Sergeant Winters. If you tell me to push these feelings you've been digging up back into their grave until you can leave your girlfriend, then I will do that. Baby, you just have to tell me what you want me to do."

"I don't want you to do anything."

"And that's the problem. I am telling you how I feel. I come home, look like a bimbo, and cook because I care, and all you tell me is something extremely passive-aggressive."

"You're not listening to me, Elaine. We're not going to be together. What we are doing is just fucking. It's sex. You want an assignment, then your orders are to abandon all hope of having more than what we have right now. I never wanted more with you." *this bitch gonna kill ya!*

Marcus decided it was time to leave. These conversations had become increasingly agitating, and he had a penchant for dishing out verbal abuse to Elaine, mainly because she could take it. And right *penchant to hit too?* now, she'd been so good to him he didn't want to unload on her. He simply wasn't interested in more with her because he hadn't closed the door on his relationship with Kendra. He didn't like the subtle pressure Elaine presented to him. He knew her feelings were growing, and he was taking full advantage of it in a selfish way. Yet, he never lied to her. He just wanted sex. He reached for his keys and started to scan for his phone. Elaine, equally frustrated, recognized his pattern and stood in front of him in protest.

"You don't have to leave, Marcus. I'm you friend first, even if I don't like what I hear. And you're in no condition to be alone. I just want to know why? Why do I have to hide in the shadows? Why are

So you can change and try to be her?

141

you not choosing me over her? Why am I not special enough to be your woman? What's the real reaso—",

"Because I just don't want you, Elaine!" he growled. "You are annoying! You've always been annoying. Your psychobabble; your opinions on everything. You were one of the most annoying women in B Company. Are you good in bed? Yes. Are you attractive? You look incredible, but you will never stop talking, for the love of God. I can't imagine what a lifetime would be like with you because the last few weeks have taught me silence is golden. You have so many opinions and are always willing—no, insistent—on sharing them as if you are the single greatest authority on life itself, when the reality is, sometimes you just need to shut the hell up!"

It was cold and harsh, but it was overdue. The one thing he was trying to avoid had been unloaded on her. He could see the angst in her face, but he couldn't stop himself. "Even during sex, you just talk and talk and talk. 'Oh, my God, Marcus, it's good? Do you like it? What do you want me to do? Are you enjoying it? Do you like it like this?' I don't know if I'm having sex or filling out a god damn questionnaire. And make no mistake, Elaine, what we're doing is strictly having sex. There is no lovemaking; no intimacy. I am here to push my dick in some orifice on your body until I no longer feel the urge to do so."

"Okay, I get it. You don't want me. You don't have to be so god damn mean about it."

She got out of the bed and walked into the kitchen. He regretted the encounter almost instantly. He wanted to apologize, but instead started to watch the next episode of *Law & Order: SVU* he'd recorded. He glanced at Elaine, who was clearly fighting back some emotion.

"Elaine, I—"

"You're not sorry, and it's okay, I understand. Dinner will be ready shortly."

He was very confused. A perfectly good girl wanted to be with him, and he didn't want her. He wasn't unhappy with her. He was just selfish, or maybe she wasn't Kendra. He'd been beating himself up for having this affair. Still, Elaine had never done anything but treat him with compassion. He got out of bed and walked into the kitchen.

Elaine was there, still in the nurse's outfit and still fighting back tears. "I'm sorry."

"It's okay, Marcus... really."

"No, it's not. I just have a lot of stress on my shoulders. I shouldn't have lashed out at you like that."

"You're dealing with a lot. I get it. I'm a tough girl, Marcus. Go lay down. Dinner will be ready soon."

He wasn't satisfied with that response, but he was the cause of it. He decided to leave well enough alone. As he walked away, Elaine spoke.

"Marcus?"

"Yeah?"

"I know I'm not perfect or pretty or even the smartest person you've ever met, but I have feelings, too, and I think sometimes you forget that. Dinner is done. I'm going to go take this off."

She walked past him into the bathroom and locked herself in. He could hear her muffled weeping behind the door.

Same asshole shit :(
I dont like it but it had to be
done. Im glad he at least
didnt hit her

CHAPTER 18
THREE'S COMPANY?

"Kendra." The voice of Mr. Baptiste echoed in her ears as she sat naked in the steel chair back in her room. She was blindfolded, as she was each night since she got here [& not the 1st night]. She could smell his cologne, Aventus by Creed, filling the night air. She imagined him wearing some variant of the crisp, long-sleeve shirt and slacks he wore every night. She could smell the wax of the lavender-scented candles, but most of all, she could smell the leather straps on her wrists and neck gently ~~pushing~~ (pulling) against her flesh. The rough fabric made her slightly moist. She wanted him, and she wanted him immediately, but by this very simple expectation, she knew she would be denied. Mr. Baptiste had a way of knowing her desires, and then punishing her for having them. He was more ~~interested in giving~~ her new desires; the unexpected. It was this curiosity more than anything that kept her coming back for more. "Kendra, are you ready?"

"Yes, Mr. Baptiste." Her voice no longer shook like it did in their initial encounter. She was aroused and excited, but as always, curious. [Girl that?] More than anything, she wanted to see what he had in store. The anticipation was killing her. When she was finally permitted to use her eyes, it was just as she imagined it. He had on a crisp, white button-

144

down shirt and dark, charcoal slacks with his Johnston & Murphy loafers. Mr. Baptiste walked toward her, circling the chair as he talked.

"Did you enjoy the restaurant the other day?"

"Yes, Mr. Baptiste."

"What did you think about the food?"

"It was good."

Pop.

She lied. She, in fact, wasn't very impressed by the food at all. She'd eaten at several nice restaurants, so nothing stood out about this one— a fact Mr. Baptiste would easily catch.

"It was... unmemorable."

"Now you're being honest. Was anything about the restaurant memorable?"

"The wait staff was nice."

"The woman in the restaurant—the waitress. Did you find her attractive?"

"I..."

Pop. The leather strap attacked her naked, bound flesh specifically her breasts, her penalty for a perceived lie. She fought back a moan to show how much she enjoyed it.

"You were about to be disingenuous, weren't you?"

"I was," she replied.

"Did you find her attractive?"

"She was a very attractive girl."

"Keep your eyes closed, Kendra." Mr. Baptiste removed the blind-fold, and she complied as he continued his inquisition.

"You've never been with a woman before, have you?"

"No, Mr. Baptiste."

"But you have thought about it?"

"Not until the other night. It was never... it isn't something I'm into." She kept her eyes closed as she heard his footsteps echo against the hard wood floors. He moved away from her before slowly moving back toward her.

"Kendra, I need you to relax and trust me. On my count, I want you to inhale as hard as you can. Three... two... one..."

She inhaled deeply, a powdery substance filling her nostrils and

Cocaine!

145

forcing her body to betray her as she coughed violently. She'd never felt this sensation before. Her eyes watered as she continued to cough.

"Breathe, Kendra," he ordered as he fed her water. Her senses disoriented themselves, and yet, she still did not open her eyes.

"What... was that?"

"A barrier remover. You've been holding on to a final layer of control, but it's time to let that go. This will help you relax."

The rush of the stimulant excited her senses. She was more alive than she'd ever been.

"Focus on the girl, Kendra."

"Amanda?"

"Yes... Amanda. You remember her name?"

"I remember everything right now."

"How did she look?"

"She was cute. Slender brunette; very perky body. A girl-next-door charm to her."

"Describe her."

"Stringy long hair, with a nice tan, no doubt because she lives out here. She didn't have a large backside. It was petite. Her breasts seem to be perky, but not fake. Pretty smile."

"What of her lips?"

"She had very... soft lips, kissable lips. They weren't full, but they weren't thin. They looked soft."

"Would you like to know if they were soft for yourself?"

"I..."

Pop.

"Do not be disingenuous."

"I would. Yes, Mr. Baptiste, I would like to know."

"Good. Kendra?"

"Yes, Mr. Baptiste?"

"Open your eyes."

She opened her eyes to see Amanda standing in front of her completely naked. She was exactly as Kendra remembered her, and seeing her nude confirmed what she imagined her body to be, with the exception of a tattoo on the right side of her torso—two Greek drama

Oop!

mask and an inscription underneath that read *Pain is pleasure.* The effects of the narcotic were kicking in.

"Take deep breaths, Kendra," Mr. Baptiste ordered. She was slow to respond. Her senses moved at an irregular pace as she tried to figure out what the substance was. Amanda walked toward her, a mischievous smile on her face. Kendra looked to Mr. Baptiste for guidance.

"Amanda, this is Mistress K. Tonight, you belong to her. Whatever she asks you to do, you will do." Amanda nodded and looked at Kendra very seductively, rapidly removing her own barriers for this new encounter.

She examined the girl, who was already moist herself. She could tell due to the lubrication building on the edges of her small thighs.

"On your knees," Kendra barked, taking a page from Mr. Baptiste's playbook.

"Yes, Mistress K." Amanda fell to her knees and crawled toward the chair. She stopped with her head right outside Kendra's thighs.

"Untie me."

The girl freed the shackles that had her mistress bound to the chair. Kendra stood up in all her splendor and walked over to the bed. Desmond took the shackles and used them to bind her to the bed. Stunned, she once again looked to him for guidance.

"But Mr. Baptiste, you told me I was in contro—"

Pop!

"You are in control of your toy. I am in control of the game," he said in his sultry voice.

She respected his authority. She wanted to fuck Amanda, who was still on her knees. She called for the young girl.

"Come here, Amanda."

"Yes, Mistress K."

Kendra lay still as the girl crawled to the bed and then on top of her.

"You're so very pretty," Amanda said as she leaned in to kiss her. The two exchanged a kiss, her lips much different than Desmond's—slim, soft, and somewhat cold. "Untie me, Amanda," Kendra ordered as she looked at Mr. Baptiste, who nodded his approval. It was her toy, after all, and she could use her in any way imaginable. She wanted to be free for this experience. She wanted control. After Amanda freed her, the girl moved her lips down to the areolas of Kendra's right breast. Kendra grabbed her by her hair and yanked her head back.

"What are you doing, girl?" Kendra barked.

"I don—"

well damn! Aggressive AF!

"If you're going to suck my titty, then suck it!" she exclaimed, forcing the girl's mouth back on her breast. She wasn't sure if this was real. The narcotic was increasing her confidence. She hardly recalled taking it at this point. All she felt was the pleasure of Amanda's lips on her bosom. The girl slowly worked her way from her right breast to her left, biting her with a slight roughness—just enough to leave a mark. The girl then took her tongue and slid it between both her breasts and worked it slowly and deliberately down to her navel.

"Are you enjoying yourself?" a deep voice asked. She almost forgot he was in the room.

"Yes, Mr. Baptiste," she moaned.

"Do you like being in control? She's yours to do with as you please."

"I do," she replied, caressing the young girl's hair.

Desmond pulled out his dick and rubbed it vigorously. At the same time, she forced Amanda's head down to the core of her body.

"Tell me who eats your pussy better," Mr. Baptiste commanded.

She could feel her heartbeat speeding up, yet she was surprisingly calm. There was no time or space. Armada licked her pussy with fervor, and yet with a gentleness that matched her soft lips and long hair. ~~Desmond continued to watch,~~ relishing the idea of Amanda's lips rubbing against Kendra's body. She wasn't prepared for this experience, but she was bound against the bed, powerless to stop it. She suddenly remembered she was not bound at all. In fact, she had told Amanda to free her. Even now, her arms pressed Amanda's head against her vagina. She had been free for quite some time—long enough to have been fully engaged in this sexual experience. Mr. Baptiste watched as Amanda pleased her, licking her in a gently intense way. Kendra laid back and started to talk. "That's right. Eat my pussy, you filthy bitch!" She thrust her pelvis into the young girl's mouth. Mr. Baptiste stood up and walked over to Kendra. "I want you to put your dick in my mouth!" she screamed. Mr. Baptiste, tired of nursing his own erection, complied.

She grabbed his hard cock and inserted it into her mouth as Amanda licked her vagina. As she sucked his chocolate pole, she moaned each time Amanda touched her most sensitive areas. She pulled his cock out of her mouth. "Go over there and fuck her from behind, and don't be nice." Mr. Baptiste once again said nothing, but stood behind the young girl within moments.

"Oh..." Amanda moaned as he entered her with his large cock. "I don't know if I can take this."

Kendra grabbed the girl by her hair and slapped her on the cheek with ferocity. "You're going to take whatever I tell you to take, you little whore. Do you understand?"

Amanda smiled and nodded. "Yes, Mistress K. I'm sorry."

Kendra slapped her on the same cheek again. "Who told you to stop licking my pussy?" She shoved her submissive's head back onto her vagina. Amanda aggressively began licking her—the same way she was being fucked from behind. Kendra moaned in sync with Desmond's thrusts into the young woman's vagina.

"Keep fucking me like that!" Amanda moaned as she began to enjoy his rod pushing deep into her pussy. Kendra shoved Amanda's head back onto her clit as she watched the dark-skinned man penetrate the young lady over and over. The entire process stimulated her.

"Is that how you look fucking me from behind?" she yelled as he continued to thrust inside her sex slave. She looked at the girl enjoying herself immensely and started to wonder how she got here. She was aggressive and submissive, excited and scared, certain and confused. She was high. She realized the substance was cocaine. Panic set in her already rapidly beating heart, now beating even faster, as if it wanted to come out of her chest. She was no longer engaged in the sexual encounter, but afraid. She pushed Amanda away and stumbled to her feet, an action which stunned both her lovers.

"Kendra, lay back down," Mr. Baptiste snarled.

"Red."

"Kendra—"

"Red. I'm going home." She gathered what she could and walked out of the suite, unaware of the fact that she was still naked. She felt Desmond's arm pull on her.

"Kendra, you don't have any clothes on!"

"What did you do to me?" she screamed as she shoved him away.

"You're having a bad trip. You need to breathe."

"This was cocaine? I want to go ho—" She stumbled forward, too weak to escape.

"It's okay. I got you," Desmond responded as she passed out in his arms.

He picked up her naked body and took her to her suite, placing her on the bed, still unconscious.

OK, this MF done got her strung out! Now she has to wait 30 dgs to pass her drug test for Huston! Did Ronnie tell him to do this as well or did he just go overboard on the drugs? I'm sure that shit was not cut!

CHAPTER 19
CLEANING HOUSE

I 'm sorry this happened the way it did. You are special to me. Marcus wrote on a card. He wasn't sure how to apologize. Elaine was a tough cookie, but his words and actions certainly hurt her. She'd been in his corner since the two began this affair, and he had done nothing but treat her as if she were a second-class citizen. Normally, he would allow her toughness to force things back to a happy medium, but after the way she expressed herself, he couldn't help but feel guilty about the way he handled things. He decided to be proactive and apologize the best way he knew how. He started cleaning up for her. The apartment was a mess, as usual, and it bothered him since she basically lived by herself. If she had kids, he could understand— or if she weren't in the military, it would make sense, but there was no excuse for her clutter. Ultimately, he decided that since they were just sleeping together, it wasn't a huge deal. Despite her comments to the contrary, he was disappointed in the lack of discipline he felt she should have carried with her from the military.

"Set the example, Winters," he said to himself. He decided it was time to show her how to properly clean again. He started in the kitchen, which took more than an hour with all the dishes in the sink and takeout containers on the counters. Typically, he didn't like using a dishwasher, but it wasn't his house, so he decided to make an exception. The more he thought about it, the more he felt guilty about the way he talked to her last time. Elaine was a sweet girl, but he didn't, in any way, want to change the nature of their relationship. In fact, the longer he stayed over her house, the more he came to appreciate Kendra. Kendra's independence separated her from Elaine, who seemed totally satisfied with being underneath him. What was more important was the fact that Kendra always either saw him for who he was, or who he could be. Elaine only saw him for who he had been. He thought he should give Kendra a call. He'd begun to miss her each day, and felt that his time with Elaine was coming to an end. The more he cleaned, the more he wrestled with the idea. Elaine was hurt, and he was apologetic for sure, but her psychobabble was getting to him. *Maybe I'm cleaning up this apartment because it's my way of putting things back the way things were in my own life. I'm sure she'd say some shit like that,* he thought mockingly. He found her glasses and put them on his face and began to cross-examine himself. "Maybe this apartment is indicative of your mind, Marcus. One moment, Kendra's the past you're ready to move on from; the next, I'm the problem because I remember you the way you were. Maybe it's time to straighten out what's real and what's just clutter," he said sarcastically as he took her glasses off and responded as himself. "I ain't got time for this psychobabble shit, Elaine."

He put the glasses back on. "But Marcus, can't you see that just like each pile of filth I have everywhere, your mind is filthy. Kendra was organized and neat and... the world made sense. You loved her 'cause it made sense, and none of the other shit you're doing makes any sense now. Marcus, you need to call her."

He took off the glasses again and thought about his conversation with himself. What had started out as a joke revealed a damning revelation. He didn't have to have a reason to love her. He just did, and when he did, the world was in order. He shrugged it off as jovial in nature and resumed his duties cleaning the kitchen, but by the time he started cleaning the bedroom two hours later, he was somewhat convinced his insight was true.

He found his headset and turned on the Bluetooth to connect to his phone. Searching for her contact information, he scrolled down to the last time he talked to Kendra. It was at the hospital, and before that it had almost been two weeks. Far too long for him to have gone without talking to her. In fact, he had never gone that long without talking to her unless he was deployed, and even then he'd send a daily email or text. He decided he needed to bridge the gap, and right now was as good a time as any. He hit 'Send' on the contact, and as the phone rang, he became more uneasy about how Kendra would respond to his call. Maybe she didn't want to hear from him. He did all but abandon her the night before her trip. He was so upset about going back to Houston, he'd all but stopped listening to the rings, until a familiar voice brought him back to the present.

"Hello?"

"KD?

"Marcus?"

It was good to hear her voice, a fact he wanted to relay immediately. But instead he held on to his ego. Bitch what?

"Sounds like you're groggy. Rough night?"

"It... I drank too much."

"Let me guess—patron?"

"I... um... yea... patron."

"I knew it. You're so predictable."

"You know me. Pre-Cal Ken. Always to my routine."

"I thought being gone would've loosened you up a bit."

"Oh... well, it might have... just a little."

"It's good to hear you. How are you doing?"

"I'm... good. How about you?"

Marcus thought about the question. He wanted to play the man with pride, but decided against it. The psychobabble was right. It was time to come clean.

"I'm.... not good, KD. I miss you."

"Marcus, I—"

"Let me finish. You had every right to question me. I've made my share of mistakes in this relationship, it's true. They all started back in Houston. I ran from my insecurities: not being able to find a job, not having a clear business plan, not being able to live up to your standards. They all bothered me. I tried to cover them up, but I began to resent you. By the time we came back to Richmond, I wanted to hurt you as bad as I was hurting. It was selfish, and I'm sorry for that. I'm sorry for being passive-aggressive. It's all been my fault."

"Marcus you didn't have to live up to my standards... you were the standard. You set my expectations, then you stopped just being who you already where."

"I didn't see it that way I guess. I wish I would have. Then maybe some of the mistakes, including the entire way I handled things in Houston, would be different."

"So... were you sleeping with someone in Houston?"

"Look, the details of the past matter, but only if you want to hear them. I'll tell you everything, but only in person. Right now, I just want you to come back home—to our home. Let's try to put together what we have because we both know that what we have is worth fighting for and working on. You're my everything, KD. I mean that shit. I'm sorry for taking you for granted; I'm sorry for everything. Can you please just come home so we can talk about it?"

The phone was silent. He wasn't sure what to expect.

"So much has changed. You hurt me, Marcus."

"I know. I'm not going to deny it."

"So, it's not as easy as just calling and saying I'm sorry."

"I didn't think it would be, but I do want to be the man you deserve."

"You know, I used to think I knew what kind of man I deserved, and that was you. The old you. Now, I'm not sure what I deserve. Did I really make you feel like you couldn't live up to my standards?"

"I don't know if you did or not, in all honesty, but there's no question I can do better. I've kind of given up on me, and I blamed you for that."

There was a silence on the phone as Kendra figured out what to say next. "I'm sorry if you ever felt like you weren't enough. You were always enough for me."

"I... thanks for saying that."

"What about my career?"

"Look, KD, you're gonna be successful with or without me, but I want you to be successful with me. I just need you to give me a second chance."

"So, what are you asking of me?"

"Come home."

"My flight... I can't just—"

"Just schedule another flight, baby. I want to see you, and I don't ever want to be without you, but we have to talk in person. If you want to finish your trip, I'm not going to stop you. But the sooner you get back to me—to us—the sooner we can get to work on our relationship. I don't want to make this too heavy, but think about it."

"Okay, I'll think about it."

"That's all I ask. Now, go enjoy yourself. I won't bother you again. Text me when you decide what you're going to do."

"Okay."

"ALRIGHT, BABY, WELL, I'LL TALK TO YOU LATER."

"Marcus?"

"Yes, KD?"

The phone was silent. He wasn't sure why she didn't want to get off the phone just yet, but he was hoping he had a chance.

"I love you."

"I love you too, Kendra."

The pair disconnected the call. It was all he needed to hear. He would have to tell her about Ronnie, and probably Elaine, but if she was willing to work on it, he could do that and survive his recent tryst. He needed to tell her about Ronnie, and soon. She was untrustworthy, and the longer he waited, the closer Kendra and Ronnie got. He wasn't sure if their relationship could survive holding on to a lie of this magnitude for this amount of time. Obviously, Ronnie was never going to tell, so he could easily just not say a word and truly work at being with Kendra, but it wouldn't work. At the end of the day, she was putting her trust in him the same way she was putting her trust in Ronnie, and it was past time for her to have all the cards. Maybe the truth would make her change her mind about everything, including him, but if he learned anything in the time she was gone, it was that he had to be the best person he could be for her in spite of his own security or desires. As he continued to clean the house, he came across the locked door of the apartment that Elaine's roommate lived in. He put Elaine's glasses back on.

"Marcus, you hiding Ronnie and me from Kendra is like this locked door. Sure, you've cleaned up the rest of your house, but in order to be fully absolved, she's needs access to all the compartments in your mind —even this locked one!" He was still ridiculing Elaine for her psychobabble, although saying it aloud made it sound more reasonable. Poignant, even. He took the glasses off and countered his own argument.

"Okay, you want honesty? I'll be honest. All doors open!" He tugged at the knob jokingly, only to find the door unlocked. He stumbled into the room. As he did, he dropped the Lysol cleaner and the steel-framed glasses in his hands, completely stunned by what he saw.

"What... in... the... hell?"

Dark room for photography?
Red Room like Mr Grey?
She in there?
Roomate tied up?

CHAPTER 20
DID THAT JUST HAPPEN?

What... in... the... hell was that? Kendra thought to herself. Did Marcus just profess his love for her? Did he apologize? Did he say the words 'I'm sorry?' It was all too much to process, especially now. She'd accepted the fact that she wanted to move on, and after one awkward night and one conversation, he'd brought everything back to the forefront. He provided a perspective he hadn't before she left. Had he said anything then near what he said now, maybe none of this would've happened. Still, she was in a different place emotionally. She wasn't sure if she was able to respond. She didn't want to go home. She was enjoying herself far too much. Yet, she needed answers. She needed some clarity, and after last night, she wasn't entirely sure the new Kendra was for her. She wasn't a drug user or a lesbian, but in one night, this Desmond had her trying cocaine and having a threesome with a woman. What's worse is that she was pretty convinced she enjoyed parts of it, possibly all of it. She enjoyed everything Mr. Baptiste had to give her. But the longer the trip went on, the less she felt like she was spending time with Desmond. Mr. Baptiste had consumed her. Still holding the phone, she texted Marcus.

Baby you're right. I love you and while I can't promise anything I do want to make this work. I'm going to change my flight plans and get out of here a little earlier. I'll see you Friday. -KD

She smiled as she hit 'Send'. It wasn't long before a text was returned to her

Us against the world -M

His text made her smile even harder. Going home seemed like a good idea after the night she had. She decided that today she'd spend the day alone. As much as she liked Desmond, she wasn't sure if she was comfortable with all that happened, and she wanted perspective; she wanted clarity. Maybe she wasn't seeing things for what they were. She had clearly made Marcus feel inadequate without trying. Maybe she was overinflating how much she really enjoyed Desmond's company. Either way, today was a day to explore the island, not the limits of her body. She got dressed for the day, donning a pastel pink and white sundress, and then cornrowed her hair to her scalp. She set out to have her first day on the island alone. She spent most of the day seeing monuments and visiting the casinos. It was a change of pace since there was no beach in sight, nor was there any rum punch. Slowly, perspective provided an answer to her time alone. She couldn't say she enjoyed it—at least not nearly as much as spending time with Desmond. She wanted to reach out to him. She needed to talk to him, but still she was determined to give herself more time. By mid-day, she was over her trip alone. Desmond would've pointed out several significant facts about the island by now. She decided that she would just go home and spend the rest of the night in bed and talk to him tomorrow.

As she got back to the hotel, the sun was beginning to set. It was, again, one of the only times she'd spent a sunset without him since she landed on Saint Martin. She got to her room and stopped.

What in the hell?

A trail of rose petals led from her doorstep to 12 E. She wanted to ignore it, but, like everything with Desmond, curiosity got the better of her. She followed the rose petals to the open door. She walked into the living quarters, but Desmond was nowhere to be found. The tub was running, however, and so she walked into the bedroom. It was clear that room service had come to clean up, and Amanda was now gone. Kendra walked into the room where a bubble bath was being drawn up and candles flickered around the bathtub. The trail of petals stopped there.

"I was hoping you would return. I wanted to apologize to you," the brisk voice said.

"There seems to be a lot of that going around today," she replied.

"Huh?"

"Nothing. What are you apologizing for?"

"It is painfully obvious you didn't enjoy our little game last night."

"What? Being tied up and drugged, then molested by a would-be lesbian? I don't think so."

"I didn't take you for that kind, but I was providing a service, and you did say you didn't want me to hold back."

"I... I did, but... damn, I didn't know."

"And I should've been more clear. That is the point of the safe word, Kendra. I always want you to feel safe around me. It's no fun for anyone if you're not enjoying it."

His words and his smile were seductive. That was how she ended up butt naked sniffing a line of cocaine while blindfolded last night.

"So you sell drugs, as well?" She wasn't sure she wanted to know the answer.

"No, but I do know how to acquire just about anything. In a party town like this, any bartender can get something illicit— for the right price, of course."

"Jeffery... of course."

"You know that's not his real name, right?"

"Close enough." They both chuckled. She looked at the tub as it filled up rapidly.

"So, is this supposed to be an apology?"

"On behalf of Desmond and Mr. Baptiste," he said with a smile. He removed his towel, exposing his nakedness. A sight she'd become accustomed to, but remained no less impressed.

"I don't want to do anything but soak with you. If you allow me to, I'll hold you, or you can sit on the other end of the tub and we can talk. And don't worry—Mr. Baptiste will not be joining us. I just want to hear about your day. It's the first one I haven't spent with you, so I'm sure there's lots to tell."

159

Umm... someone lock the front door please

She thought about his request. Since this would be one of her final days on the island, it made sense to take him up on it. She'd spent the entire trip with him and had decided that, although she did have work to do when she returned home, there was no work necessary for her to spend time with Desmond. She slid off the pink and white pastel summer dress and stepped into the water. She wasn't sure if she wanted to be held by him. The tub was big enough for both of them to sit facing each other.

"Please." He beckoned her, extending his hand. It settled the debate. She moved underneath his massive, firm chest as he held her.

"I'm sorry," he said again. He kissed her on the forehead dissolving some of her defenses.

She sat silently in the water before she finally said, "My trip is almost over."

"I thought you had another week?"

She didn't want to tell him the truth, so she lied.

"Work called. I have to go in earlier than expected."

"That is terribly unfortunate." He was silent for a moment, but he had learned to read her all too well. "So, are you going to work things out with Marcus?" His words brought back her reality. She got out of the tub, reached for a towel, and walked into the bedroom. Desmond promptly followed her. "Kendra... why did you leave? Why are you running?"

"I'm not run—"

"Before you say that, know that I understand you very well. Now, why? Was it what I said?"

She knew her silence only confirmed that she had indeed thought about Marcus.

"So, you're going to work things out with—"

"I don't know."

"What is there not to know?"

"What is going on with us, Des? Is this all service, or is there something more to us?"

"Are you serious?"

"I'm very serious."

"Unbelievable."

"Really? How so, Desmond? I just can't tell. One minute I think we're making a connection, and then you're fucking my brains out. Was this real, or just part of the service?"

"I don't want your money, Kendra."

"Then what do you want?"

"I... want..."

"What, Des? What do you want? I tell you I'm leaving and all you have to say is 'that's unfortunate'? Are you even going to miss me?"

"Kendra, I want... you. I miss you even when you're right next to me. I'm jealous of that pillow on that bed for being able to hold your head all night long. I want you spiritually, physically, mentally. I want us. I know the chemistry we're creating right now isn't something I'm imagining. You gotta feel it, too. And yeah, neither one of us planned this, but by my count, it doesn't seem like anything we do plan works out well. But how does that sound? You were on vacation; this was supposed to be a fling. But it isn't, not anymore. Not to me."

"So, what are you asking me?"

"I'm asking you to take a chance on us... on love." *Nigga Please! You are too deep in the game! Ronnie really getting her moneys worth*

His words were sharp, meaningful, and exact. For the first time in her life, she felt valued beyond measure. This wasn't just having fun anymore. This wasn't a late-night creep. This wasn't even the mundane, slightly above-average sex she and Marcus would have. With this final statement, he confirmed what she'd been trying to deny to herself the majority of her trip. This was love like she never thought possible. *this is lust* Like she had never experienced before, and that terrified her. All her other relationships before this were in vain. His words shook her bones and made her heartbeat elevate. She parted her full lips to gasp for oxygen. That was the only invitation he needed to meet her lips with his own. He kissed her to cement everything he had just put into her spirit. *This is love.* Words she couldn't pry from Marcus. At this moment, she couldn't care less about him. She was with him—not the man she was paying for companionship, or the cultural expert on all things Saint Martin. This wasn't even Mr. Baptiste. This was Desmond. The real Desmond, and he was in love with her the way she was in love with him, even if she had been trying not to acknowledge it this entire time.

He took her into his bulging arms and kissed her on her neck. She welcomed the kisses as an invitation to the rest of her body. She yearned to have his lips intrude upon her again and again. Every connection made her feel alive and valued. She caressed his chocolate scalp as he ran his lips from her earlobe to the side of her neck. The scent of his natural, washed skin intoxicated her, and she yearned for him to slip inside her, but instead he connected his lips with hers again, kissing her very gently, then more vigorously, until the two became one.

She opened her eyes to see if this was real, the moisture on his full lips combining with the sugary taste of his tongue. It might as well have been her first kiss because she would never forget this moment. She was certain this was how love was supposed to feel. And she was willing to comply, not because it was expected of her by Mr. Baptiste, or because she was revealing some secret erotic fantasy. No, she complied because she wanted him as badly as he wanted her. She was willing to open her spirit and allow him to pour love into her, a feeling she desperately wanted, needed, and wouldn't forsake regardless of how she found it. *Girl you are going to get hurt! He is a player.*

"Kendra, you are beautiful." It was a declaration of his love. Although he had said the words many times before, the way he said it this time gave them deeper meaning. She meant much more to him than a sexual object, or an experiment in liberation. As he laid her on the bed, she realized that this was the night they would love each other, and he soon entered her without hesitation. There was majesty in each stroke, filling her with the passion and bliss only love could bring. They kissed as if their lips lit the night sky. This was undeniable.

"Give me all of you," she whispered in his ear as he continued to pulsate inside her. His body moved to the rhythm as if it were making the candlelight around them dance. He dwelled within her, pressing deeper with sensitive, caressing stokes. This wasn't for the sport, but rather the spirt. *Oooh!! Fire!* It was for the connection they had built over the past few weeks. This was for *snow cones*. Her breasts touched his chest as they made eye contact during the entire experience.

"I love you, Kendra."

She extended her legs to allow him to enter her unrestricted. He gently continued to push his rod into her as she closed her eyes momentarily, feeling the pleasure provided by him, not wanting to forget a second of this moment. As the rhythm picked up, it became more difficult to maintain eye contact. She was close to having an orgasm, and as badly as she wanted to stay with him, her physical reaction was uncontrollable. She held on for as long as she could, digging her nails into his perfectly carved flesh, but it was a losing battle as she began to cum. But it didn't matter because so did he. For one brief moment, they experienced love and ecstasy at the same time. It seemed as if their moans were actually in sync as they reached the pinnacle of pleasure. When he was done, he didn't slump his body onto hers, but used his remaining strength to gently ease himself next to her. "I've never felt this way before," he said, confirming all that she experienced wasn't in her own head. There were no more words to be spoken. None had to be. Tonight, love was made.

You know she pregnant now right?
No condoms 2-3 wks?

CHAPTER 21
HERO WORSHIP

"I can't believe this!" He was stunned by what he saw. The room was devoid of human presence—no bed, no clothes, and no indication that anyone lived there. Instead, there were pictures of him everywhere in this room, along with a giant canvas half painted of him in his military uniform. He sat down to examine the photos, many of which were from his time in the Army. But there were also more recent ones; ones that he'd never seen before. Ones he couldn't have possibly posed for. He continued to scan the pictures, trying to comprehend what was going on. Was he part of some sort of military operation he didn't know about? Why would Elaine have so many photos of him? He looked around and saw the black leather journal, the one she'd taken all the therapy notes in. He picked it up and opened it to read one of the entries:

Marcus loves my new breasts. For 4 grand a pop, he should! He doesn't even know I got these for him, since he loves breasts so much. You have to keep your man happy right? It would've been hard to turn these down. I was nervous that maybe I went too large because I really didn't know Kendra's size, but I didn't need to. I hate saying that name. I wish he never met that tramp. I

This Bitch is obsessed.

shouldn't call her that – she's probably a nice girl. After all, he seems to like her and he can't be wrong so maybe she is nice. But he needs a woman. He needs me. He'll appreciate my sacrifices one day. One day when our kids look back on this they'll laugh. They'll say, "Mommy, who is Kendra?" and I'll say "Someone significant to your dad, but she doesn't matter now 'cause I married him." I'll be Mrs. Sgt. Marcus Winters. I love that name. I love our life!

HE DROPPED THE BOOK AND A PICTURE FELL OUT. HE BENT OVER TO pick it up. There was an old military photo of him at a dinner with Kendra, only she had been removed from the picture and Elaine Photoshopped into the portrait. It was the ultimate confirmation. "This bitch is crazy!" he said aloud. This had nothing to do with a military op, or even therapy. Elaine was obsessed with him. He turned to leave, only to find Elaine back early from her trip to the store.

"Marcus, wait, I can explain," she said in panic.

"You can explain what? You following me? This... shrine? I don't know what to call it. This is psycho shit!"

He walked around her and headed into the living room, proceeding to the door. She sprinted past him and blocked the door with her body.

"Wait a second! Please, just... just hear me out for a second! Please!" He started to make his way toward her and the door. Elaine put a hand up in protest, reaching for her purse with the other one. He paused, remembering the pistol she kept on her.

He stood there, totally unsure of what the woman he'd been spending time with would do next.

"Marcus, look, okay, so would you just please hear me out!"

"What in the fuck, Elaine! You've been stalking me!"

"No. It sounds crazy when you say it like that, but—"

"That's 'cause it is crazy! What the h—"

"I'm not crazy!" she screamed at the top of her lungs, digging deeper into the purse. He was certain she had her weapon. "Stupid, Elaine. Stupid, stupid, stupid! He's never going to love you now. You're ruining everything!" she said to herself as she sobbed and paced in front of her living room door, holding the purse. Marcus wasn't sure what to say. The therapist needed therapy. She seemed to be falling apart before his eyes. She looked at him, realizing he was watching her talk to herself, and tried to regain some of her dwindling composure.

"I'm... *not*... crazy. This is bigger than that. We are bigger than that. Listen, please, just listen. Since I first met you back when I was a private, I knew there was something about you. Something magical. When you chose me out of all the girls in B Company to share your burdens with, I knew you felt the way I felt. When we're together, it makes sense. I know you feel it. I know you want me. The way you touch me, it's not just sex. It can't be. I've given everything to you. I've nursed you back to health. I've been a shoulder for you to cry on. I watch that stupid Law & Order show you like so god damn much when it's terrible. I've been your therapist and your whore. But I thought you would see that Kendra never loved you—not the way you deserve. You deserve better; you deserve far more than anything she can give you. Than any woman can give you. You deserve me. You need a cook, I'll cook for you. You need a slut, I'll do any dirty thing you can imagine. You need someone to help you be the man I know you can be, I'll do it. You just have to tell me what you want, and I'll do it. Don't you understand? It's because I love you. It's all because I love you! Just... please... please don't leave me. Don't leave what we've been working on."

He stood there as she talked. He said nothing. As she cried frantically, he thought about all the breadcrumbs she'd been leaving. *Boy, when you fuck up, you really fuck up good, Winters.* He looked back at her. She was still in a state of paranoia, and he knew he had to calm her down.

"Why do you have your purse, Elaine?"

"What? I... I'm not sure what you're asking."

"It's pretty simple. Why is your hand in your purse?"

"Marcus, just—"

"I may not be a therapist, or have all these accreditations, but I do know what a combatant looks like when their hand is on a firearm."

"No, Marcus. No! No! No! This is coming out all wrong!"

Her pupils were dilating. He needed to act fast if he wanted to survive this encounter.

"I believe you, Elaine, I do—"

"Don't you fucking dare patronize me! You don't think I know what you're doing? I'm a god damn therapist! I know when someone is bullshitting me, Marcus."

"I'm not bullshitting you, Elaine. I can't bullshit you. Come on now, like you said, you've nursed me back to health and you've picked my brain. I've been on the fence about Kendra since before you and I hooked up, but I'll be honest, this isn't helping. Look, if you want to have this talk for real, you'll take you (your) hand out of your purse and I'll go sit on the couch."

He slowly walked backwards toward the couch, not taking his eyes off her. She wiped the tears from her eyes as mascara smeared her pale cheeks. She put the purse back on the counter. He gently ushered her toward the couch where their sessions took place.

"I wasn't going to shoot you, Marcus. I just wanted you to—"

In an instant, he grabbed her with one of the military compliance techniques he knew and pressed her against the wall.

"You crazy bitch! You tried to pull a gun on me?"

"I didn't! I swear!"

"Holt, I should report you to the M.P.'s right now. I could have you court martialed for what you've done, and believe me, I still have enough pull around here to get that, or much worse, done to you. So, I'm going to say this as a courtesy for all the times we've had: get some mental health and stay the fuck away from me! And if you ever, and I mean ever, think about pulling a pistol on me, I'll make sure it's your very last thought. Now, are we clear, Corporal?"

"Marcus, please! I—" He pulled her wrist even tighter.

"Are we clear, Corporal Holt?"

"Yes... Sarge."

He released her, and she turned around, holding her now aching wrist. He glared at her, repressing his rage. As he walked out, he decided to provide one final answer to her myriad of questions.

"You asked me once what Kendra has that you don't. Well, the answer is sanity, you insecure, delusional motherfucker."

He walked out of the house and slammed the door, not looking back.

WOW!, Thats crazy
I wald have took the gun though—
She might kill herself or come after
you later

CHAPTER 22
IF IT ISN'T LOVE

Kendra opened her eyes to scan the room, but her lover wasn't there. She laid there, naked and happy as the sun pierced the window, kissing her chocolate skin. "Des?" she said aloud. There was no answer. She looked at the time—8:35. Her flight was at two. She regretted changing the flight after the night she had with Desmond, but she had to resolve her confusion one way or another. Getting out of bed, she slid on the red-laced Victoria Secret panties laying on the floor she wore the night before.

"Des?" she repeated. Still no answer. She located the hotel robe and tied it while walking from the bedroom to the suite's living area. Desmond sat outside shirtless with his black briefs on, eating his salmon and egg-white breakfast. She looked at his structure, his flesh tightly wrapped around his dark-chocolate skin, each muscle contracting at the slightest movement. He was living art. She noticed her plate of scrambled eggs, croissant, and turkey bacon sitting in a glass case to keep it warm.

"It just got here, so it's pretty warm," he said. She walked onto the patio, took the seat directly across from him, and uncovered her food. She was hungry, true, but she was in no mood to eat. There was too much to talk about, and this was the final day of their time together.

She wanted to know if last night was real. She knew what he said, but there were a lot of emotions. She knew it was love, but she still needed confirmation. His primary job was to provide pleasure to women, and maybe this was all a part of the service. If it was, she had to know. Did everything he said, everything he did, mean something more to him than casual, or even erotic, sex? More importantly, did he truly feel the way she felt? She wanted to spend the entire day with him discussing this, but she knew this day, like all days she'd ever enjoyed, would pass too quickly. There was no time for her to build up to her point the way she normally would, so she took the direct approach.

"So, about last night..."

"What about it?" he replied. She could smell the scent of last night's sex on him. Looking at his body, it all slightly aroused her. *Focus, Kendra.*

"It... felt different." Her attempt at being direct failed. It was all she could get out.

"What did it feel like?"

"It felt like something more than pleasure. It felt like more than sex. It felt like—"

"Like what?"

"Love. It felt like love. I don't want to presume we were in an emotional place over the last couple of days. We said a lot of things to one another. Is this love?"

There was silence. Desmond continued to push his food around his plate as if contemplating her words. Kendra looked at him, the man who removed her sexual prudishness. The man she paid for pleasure. The man she had, in many ways, kept more distant than anyone, but who somehow stumbled past her barriers, hurdled her guards, and landed inside her heart. There was no more denying it. Still, he was silent.

"If you tell me right now that this was just part of the game, then I will accept that, but I don't want to play anymore. Last night felt different. I feel different. This morning, the way our eyes are connecting at this very moment, feels different, and I need to know if what you said is true. Is this love?"

He looked away, wiping his mouth with the white linen cloth, his thoughts visibly betraying him. He held the napkin to his mouth much longer than he should have, as if wiping away the idea she had just planted in his head. Kendra waited, anticipating his response, hoping they could, at the very least, begin a dialogue—a real dialogue about last night. A dialogue about the things she was saying that he hadn't yet denied. About love. About a future together. He closed his eyes, his voice strong and piercing.

"Let's just stick to our regimen. Now eat your meal." The words cracked the patches on her already delicate heart. She wanted to retreat. The old her would have certainly retreated, but her voice rebelled against her as she let her thoughts spill into the open space between them.

"I'm not talking to you," she said confidently as she stood up and walked closer to the man she'd spent the last few weeks with.

"Kendra, sit down and eat your meal," he repeated.

She fired back vehemently, "I'm not talking to you, Mr. Baptiste. I am here for Desmond." She walked in front of him and straddled his lap. He tried to look away, but she gently placed her hand on his face, turning it back to hers. "You've spent the past few weeks getting to know my body, my mind, my heart. You've helped me face my fears. I've been your submissive, dormant, plaything willing to do anything you ask, but when you scrape someone's car, you leave as much paint as you take. I know the sound of your voice as well as my own. I know Mr. Baptiste when I hear him because you've trained me to know, but I'm not here for him. I'm here for you, Desmond. The real Desmond. In such a short period of time, you've managed to learn everything about me, and I'd like to think I've picked up a thing or two about you—the real you— during this time. I'm asking you a question, face to face, woman to man. Do I complete you? Is any of what you said last night true? Is this love?"

His eyes gave her the answer. She knew his heart. The answer was yes, whether he admitted it or not. She was certain. Moreover, she was certain he knew she was certain. There, for the first time since they met, Desmond Baptiste was exposed and vulnerable, and it didn't matter because so was she. The two of them sat there cradling the fragility of their hearts, hoping the other wouldn't break it. She wanted to kiss him, but feared it would only make him regain his strength and ruin the moment. This man had unleashed her womanhood and taught her how to be loved in order to truly give love. For the first time in her life, she was comfortable in her own skin. For the first time in her life, she realized her true value.

She stood up and walked around the back of the chair he was sitting in. She whispered in his ear. "Desmond, I don't care who you were before last night. I know it should matter, but it doesn't, because last night I fell in love with you. Hell, maybe I fell in love with you the moment I agreed to do any of this. All I know is that I don't want to let this feeling go. I don't want to let go what we've been building. It's only been a few weeks, and it's already more powerful than anything I've felt in my lifetime."

"How do you know it's not infatuation?" he asked calmly.

"Because I've been infatuated, and it doesn't make me want to be a better person. It doesn't make me want to give up everything I have for something new. It doesn't make my heart beat like this. I don't think I want to be with you, I know I do." She could see it in his eyes he loved her. And there was no doubt, as she leaned in to kiss him, that his eyes looked away. As she tugged his face to establish eye contact again, she was stunned by what she saw. His eyes came back cold. This wasn't her lover.

"Kendra, you don't know me at all. We barely know each other. You can't possibly mean what you're saying right now."

"Don't tell me that. Don't discredit the way I feel. I know your heart. I feel it beating even now in sync with my own. Just tell me you don't love me, Desmond Baptiste, and I won't say anything else about the subject."

He was silent. His eyes shifted downward. *Say something, damn it,* Kendra thought to herself. *Say anything, please.*

"Kendra, you're in a relationship. You needed a break; I gave you that break. All of your words sound wonderful right now, but the fact is you decided to pay for a service, and now that service has been provided. It's not fair to make this more than what it has been. You gotta know when you get back on that plane, Marcus—that's right, your boyfriend—is going to be waiting for you. He's going to try to fix your relationship."

His words were dousing. Marcus was still waiting at their home, a reality she had all but forgotten. A reality that didn't matter to either of them the night before.

"I want you to go back home, look him in the eyes, and end it, if you can. If you can make that decision independent of this, then we can talk about a future."

His answer was cold, but truthful. Regardless of how she felt, she had unresolved issues. Marcus, despite his recent behavior, deserved better than to be disregarded. It was a reality she didn't want to face. Her desires had gotten the better of her.

"You can tell room service to come get the food. I've lost my appetite," she uttered before walking away from the patio and into the living room. She thought about her time in Saint Martin and all the wonderful moments she created with Desmond. She knew it was a break from reality, and for a second, for one brief pause in existence, she thought she found what so many had truly tried to attain—clarity. He was so committed to her not even half a day earlier, and now he wasn't. She felt there had to be more to his about-face, more to his sudden coldness, but Desmond's words were so sharp they tainted the entirety of her trip. She wanted to go home. She didn't want to be around him a second longer. She decided to take a shower to forget their conversation.

She went into the shower and took off her robe and her panties. She let the water rush against her naturally curly hair, and as she closed her eyes, her tears mingled with the water. That's when she heard him again.

"I care, about you, Kendra. I just want to make sure you are available, and this isn't a fleeting thing."

"The fact you have to question that says you don't know me at all."

"That's just it—I don't know you. Not like I thought I did."

"What are you talking about? You know everything about me. Hell, you taught me!" There was a brief silence. Kendra opened her eyes and turned to face him in the shower.

"Your phone last night kept flashing. I was trying to power it off when the pop up went into your text. You just told Marcus you loved him, and you can't wait to see him. You also told him you changed your flight, but you told me it was a work thing."

She was stunned. The one moment she felt any doubt about Desmond—the events after the threesome—had come back to bite her.

"Desmond, it wasn't like that. We had—"

"Thing is, I get it. I can't expect you to turn your life upside down, especially for what we're doing, but don't sit here and stand on sanctimony, as if you're fully committed to us, or whatever you want to call what we're doing, because you're not."

His words rang true, even if he read that text by accident, and it was out of context. The fact of the matter was she wasn't sure how she'd respond to Marcus after actually seeing him. There was no question she was in love with Desmond, but that didn't mean she didn't also have feelings for the man she spent the last six years with.

The two sat quietly in the shower as the water ran against their bodies. Kendra wanted to explain how wrong he was, but she wasn't sure why she sent that text. She wasn't sure about anything at the moment. She wanted to say something to reassure him he had it all wrong, but instead, she put her guard up.

"I'll send your money through PayPal, so you don't have to worry about that."

It was the worst possible response. She turned back around and buried her face in the water.

"Thanks. We should get cleaned up, and when you're ready, I'll take you to the airport."

He got out of the shower. There was no need to continue their conversation. Reality had bitterly introduced itself to their vacation paradise.

Seconds later, she got out of the shower and went back to her suite. She dressed herself in a low-cut, Marc Jacobs, teal summer dress, along with matching sandals. She glanced at the handmade seashell necklace Desmond made her one afternoon, wrestling with the idea of wearing it, and eventually deciding against it. Desmond might appreciate it, but more than likely he would find it insulting, as if she were trying too hard. She wouldn't be wearing it because she wanted to; she would be wearing it to get him back.

There was less time than she anticipated after showering and getting ready to actually get to the airport. She packed her bag and was ready to leave. The silence in the house was nothing compared to the silence of the car ride. The entire thing reminded her of her last day with Marcus and how silent they both were then. *Fuck... Des is right. What am I doing?* The triangle was too much to bear. The 'what happens' rule was all she could think about. Maybe it was best to just let things die a natural vacation death. When she got to the airport, Desmond helped her with her luggage, as well as his own. — He's leaving too!

Say something to him, damn it! Tell him how you're not giving up on this. Tell him how much he means to you. Tell him you're sorry for not being honest. Tell him you're sorry for the PayPal thing. Just say something! She said nothing. Instead, she continued as if nothing had happened between them.

As they walked past the security checkpoint, their gates were located on opposite sides of the airport. Now was as good a time as any to say goodbye. She turned to him and forced herself to speak.

"You're right."

"Huh?"

"I'm not sure what I want. This was fun, Des, but I have a life back home. Goodbye. I had a great time."

She kissed him on the cheek and turned around, walking off without looking back, fighting the urge to cry all the way to the plane.

"Kendra!"

She never stopped. Reality was only two and half hours away.

CHAPTER 23
THE RESULTS ARE IN

"**M**r. Winters, Doctor Packard will see you now."
Marcus had been hesitant to make an appointment, but he felt that after some of the recent issues he'd been experiencing, it was time to get the results of his blood work. He'd been careless with Elaine, and while she was crazy as hell, he did trust her on some level to be clean, yet the drunken nights, hidden condoms, and above all her recent outburst, made him apprehensive. Deciding to work things out with Kendra, he wanted to have a clean slate—as clean as could be, given that he hadn't bothered to tell her about Ronnie up to this point. There was no way he could tell her about Elaine—not after the fiasco she put on. He just figured he should start over, for real this time. *You been fucking up, Marcus. You gotta do better.*

The doctor came in, a concerned look on his face. A look that made Marcus instantly regret having any trust in Elaine's crazy ass. "What do I have, Doc?" he said without hesitation. Doctors don't come in with that look on their face and have good news.

"Mr. Winters, I want you to know the results of your blood work came back with no sexually transmitted diseases."

Marcus was relieved to hear that, but the doctor still seemed concerned. "That's great news, Doc. So, why do you still have that look on your face?"

The doctor took the chair next to Marcus and looked him in his eyes. "Mr. Winters... Marcus... as you know, we ran a lot of tests, and as is standard protocol, we check for everything. High blood pressure, chronic illnesses, just about anything you can imagine. I'm sorry to tell you this, but after running these test, then re-running them, we've determined several things, the most alarming of which are your dopamine levels. They are significantly low for a man your age."

"Okay, so what does that mean to me in plain English?"

"There's not a good way to say this, but—"

"Damn it, Doc! Just spit it out!"

"It appears you have a very rare version of Parkinson's Disease."

The doctor was still talking, but Marcus had completely stopped listening. It was a ton of bricks hitting him in the chest. His military training helped him prepare for bad news, but he was still shocked, confused, and scared. After a few moments, he was able to gather himself. The doctor, who clearly had a hard time delivering the news, was still talking when Marcus interrupted him.

"Okay, so there's no cure for Parkinson's, but there is medicine. When can I start treatment?"

"Mr. Winters, I'm afraid it's a bit more complicated than that. Your symptoms aren't that of a regular patient with Parkinson's. This particular strand is a variant that only happens in the smallest fraction of the world's population. It's highly aggressive, and no known medicines combat it. It's... it's..."

"What is it, Doc?"

"There is a high mortality rate with it. It's aggressively lethal, Mr. Winters."

"Are you telling me I'm dying?"

"I'm sorry, Mr. Winters." We all die. Just some faster than others

Marcus fought back tears. All his time complaining about making something out of his life. All his time fighting with Kendra, hiding his relationships with Ronnie and Elaine—it was all pointless now. He looked at the doctor, desperate for answers.

"How long do I have?"

The doctor looked at his clipboard again and flipped several pages. "Keep in mind that Parkinson's itself is a rare disease which we know little about, and we know even less about this particular strand. We know close to nothing, but in the best-case scenario, you have about five years. The average, however, has been less than two."

Marcus froze, the tears welling up in his eyes. He stood up and took a giant breath.

"Some luck, huh, Doc? I survived Afghanistan. I was the commanding officer of a platoon with zero casualties. I've been shot at so many times I thought I was immortal. And to be taken out like this?"

"Mr. Winters, I—"

"I know what you're going to say, Doc, but you can save it. I just need to get out of here. Thanks for seeing me."

He abruptly walked out of the building. No one followed him. He figured the doctor realized how heavy the news was. After all, he would need the doctor before the doctor needed him. All he could think about was Kendra. He had been so self-absorbed, so calculating, selfish, and spiteful—which was why he ended things with Elaine. But never did he think he was going to be leaving her alone. He loved her and always did. He, like so many other men before him, lost his way at some point. There was only one thing for him to do, and that was the one thing he felt got him out of so many firefights in Afghanistan. Something he hadn't done since he left the military. He prayed. *Lord, I don't know how much time you're gonna give me, and you and I both know I don't deserve another chance, but If you allow me to, I want to spend every single moment making this woman the luckiest woman on the planet. I don't know if it's in your plans, but can you please let me spend my remaining days married to the best woman I've ever met?* Why? The one you hurt the most?

He stopped the car and broke into tears. His once bright, if later uncertain, future was over. He was foolish to ever try to hurt the one person who was there to lift him up. "Come on, soldier, get it together," he said to himself. But it wasn't enough. The tears refused to cease, flowing from his eyes. He thought about how he first felt joining the military, and how he felt when he met Kendra. He'd been a major disappointment to himself after leaving the military, but she never treated him as such. Not like he treated himself for not being the man he knew he was capable of being. For not standing on his own two feet and providing for his woman and his family. And she was his family. He looked in the rearview mirror of his car to make eye contact with himself and wipe his eyes. A feeling he hadn't felt in years rushed over him, and his urge to cry was gone. His pride had kicked in. He pointed his index finger at the reflection. "You're not going to die on your knees, Sergeant Winters. You are not going to die in some hospital bed begging for life to end. You are going to live like you mean it. You will leave this earth with your shit together because 'You are Bravo Company! And Bravo doesn't quit! Bravo doesn't surrender! Bravo doesn't fail! Bravo fights!'"

It was a mantra Rodriguez had been trying to convince him of for some time now. He looked in his wallet. *Seventy-two dollars. Fuck.* He looked at his gas needle. It was already on 'Empty'. *I'll spend five on gas. It's gonna have to do.* He looked at the time. Kendra's plane would land in the next hour and a half. He pulled into the gas station and put five dollars into his tank and started the car back up. It barely moved the needle. *Can't worry about that now.* He drove over to Richmond Floral and walked in. There was a slender, elderly lady at the counter. He walked up to her, passing the scrubs and several exotic floral arrangements.

"Hello. How can I help you?"

"How are you? I'm looking for a dozen purple roses."

"We have those."

The woman walked to the cooler where all the colored flowers were located and pulled out a bushel of purple roses. She started to unravel them. Marcus looked around at the prices of roses with baby's breath. *$28.93. Perfect.* The lady put the roses in a vase and added water, then the baby's breath. When she was finished, she rang up the total. "That will be $53.27."

"Excuse me?"

"The total for the roses is $53.27."

He glanced at the red roses, then turned back.

"Why are those roses twenty-nine dollars and these almost twice as much?"

"Purple is a difficult color to find, so they are more expensive."

"I just walked back there with you. You had five bushels of these back there!"

"Yes, sir, I know, and they are all $53.27."

Marcus put his head down in frustration. *If I get these roses, there's no way I'll be able to get the rest of the stuff I want to get. Fuck!*

He looked around and saw a few buckets with roses that had already bloomed, including some purple roses. They were on discount. The question came to him.

"So, now that you've opened this bushel, what happens when these roses go bad?"

"We sell them at a discount."

"How much are the discounted roses?"

"A dollar-fifty each."

Marcus walked over to the discounted roses. A few of them were beyond saving, but many of them had only a few bad rose petals on them. He began to search for the roses. One, two, three, he picked them, and they were in decent shape. After twenty minutes of searching, he was able to find eleven purple roses he could salvage. He wanted twelve, and so he looked over the roses one more time until he found one that looked extremely fragile. He picked it up and brought it over to the lady who seemed somewhat agitated by his presence at this point. She counted the roses, handling them with no consideration. When she picked up the last rose, he found the head snapped off the flower. Marcus bit his tongue. He was frustrated with the lady.

"Oops, sorry," the lady said nonchalantly.

Damn it, lady, you know how hard it was to find twelve of your bullshit overpriced roses!

He thought about the white rose that was in the discount bucket. It was vibrant and strong. He jogged back over and grabbed the rose and brought it back.

"Put this one in the middle." The lady took the rose and added it. The bad petals were still on these roses, but he decided he'd pull them off when he got home.

"Your total is $19.42," the lady said.

He pulled out a twenty and gave it to her.

That worked out even better than I thought it would, he thought as he was took the roses to his car. He'd still need a vase, but he had one at home, so he wasn't too concerned with that. He was more flustered by the fact he had spent so much time in the flower shop. The one thing he didn't want to waste ever again was time. It was too valuable, and he didn't want to spend even a second doing something pointless. But picking each rose and making sure they looked good once he removed the old petals was worth it for Kendra. He'd be cutting it close to pick up everything else he wanted to get for her, but he still went to the local grocery store and picked up a couple of lavender-scented candles, as well as catfish, greens, yams, and cornbread mix. He topped it all off with a bottle of Wild Horse Cabernet—all of her favorites. I*t's not Momma J's, but it's gonna work.*

He pulled into the driveway and opened the car door, taking the food and wine inside. He seasoned and prepared the meal based on an online recipe he once found that said it was close to Momma J's. The fried catfish would take no time, but the greens and yams and cornbread would take a bit longer. He had just finished seasoning the catfish when he remembered he left the flowers in the car. When he opened the car door, he began picking damaged petals off the flowers until they were perfect. He pulled each one, one by one, and put them in a plastic bag in his car when he heard his name.

"Marcus?"

He couldn't believe it. Elaine was standing in front of his home. Their home. He became livid.

"Elaine... are you serious? Right now? What in the hell are you doing here?"

"You weren't answering my calls. I wanted to talk."

"You have got to be the looniest toon on the planet. There is nothing to talk about. I told you this shit was over. Now get the fuck out of here."

"My God, Marcus, how can you be such an asshole to me? I've let you do things to me no one has."

"Elaine, this is so far out of bounds I can't even tell you what I'm feeling right now, but you need to go before shit gets ugly."

"Are those flowers?"

"Get the fuck out of here!"

"I can't believe this shit. I love you, while this woman hasn't done anything but take you for granted. She denies you sex, accuses you of things, makes you feel less than a man... and she gets flowers! I do everything for you, including fix your broken relationship with her, and all I get is to swallow your cum!"

"Elaine, I'm only going to say this once: I don't want you. I never did. Yes, Kendra accuses me of things, but that's because I've done them. As far as you and I go, we fucked, but putting aside the fact you need medication, this is yet another reason why I don't want you. When we first started this, you just wanted dick. I gave you that. Now I'm not gonna do that anymore, but I'm gonna make this real simple for you. You're on my property, and If I see you come here again, I'm gonna get my gun and shoot you. Do you understand?" Wow!

He watched as her skin turned bright red and her eyes filled with rage.

"I fucking hate you, Marcus!"

"I'm sorry this is ending this way, but it's gotta end. I gotta fix my relationship. Now, if you care about me at all like you say you do, you'll get out of here... now!"

He didn't mean a word of it, but Elaine was already angry and unstable. The last time he called her crazy, he almost took a bullet, so he decided to reach her in the fantasy world she built for herself and let her down as easy as he could. He slowly walked in the house and locked the door. *This crazy motherfucker here.* He seriously considered calling the police, but he couldn't risk things escalating before Kendra came home. Besides, he'd just gotten the most defining news of his life. It was ending, and too damn soon. *No time for drama.*

He looked at the time. Kendra was certainly off the plane by now. He knew his time was limited. He laughed at the thought. *My time is limited... the irony.* He wanted to break down. He wanted comfort; any comfort. A part of him even wanted it from Elaine, but Kendra was on her way. He started to look for the purple vase for the flowers. There was a clear glass vase she'd kept from the first time he sent her a dozen roses, which seemed like a more symbolic gesture. He knew Kendra would recognize the vase because it held sentimental value, but also because there was a slight crack in the vase from the time it slipped out of his hands into the sink too hard.

He took the vase and placed the flowers and baby's breath in there, leaving the white rose in the center. He meticulously pruned the wilted petals again, making sure they were strong and vibrant.

"Perfect," he said after nine minutes and countless petals.

He checked the catfish nuggets. He fried a few to see if they came out well. Marcus was a decent cook, but his real strength in the kitchen came because he could follow directions better than most. He tried the first one. "Not bad." He added onion powder and garlic salt to the recipe to make it a bit more flavorful. When he was done, he tried another one. "Oh, shit, Winters," he said, impressed by his work. He grabbed the bottle of Wild Horse and put it in the freezer. "She'll like it chilled." He then took the candles and put them on the kitchen table. He was about to light the first one when his hand shook uncontrollably. He dropped the lighter and sat down on the kitchen floor. He let out a giant scream as he fought back tears again. He told himself he couldn't—Kendra was on her way home. He needed to get it together in order to have the conversation they needed to fix this relationship. *Whatever it takes, Marcus, whatever it takes.* Thinking of Kendra did the trick, keeping the tears away, until, before long, he regained control of his extremities and could light the candles. Kendra would be home soon.

And Elaine is lurking outside to welcome her home too! Stupid! You didn't check to see if she left!

CHAPTER 24
WELCOME TO THE VA, PART II

The plane landed early, and Kendra powered on her phone. As she checked it, she realized there were no missed calls. It disappointed her, so she checked her voicemail just in case the icon simply didn't indicate there was a call. There were none. She was home, and it was time to make a true decision on going to Houston. Yet, she couldn't help but think of Desmond. Was it all just business? Was there more to their time together, or was this the separation she needed for her to clear her head and be the woman Marcus wanted her to be? She loved him, it was true, but no one made her feel like Desmond. She closed her eyes and tried to remember his touch, his smile, his scent on her skin. She longed for it. She wanted to call Desmond, but decided against it, since her last conversation seemed callous and uncaring. She knew he was hurt by her deception, and rightfully so. But there was too much to explain. She wanted to put him in her rearview mirror. This was her life. Marcus was her life. Their trial separation was over. She didn't want to leave him in the past, and although her inability to speak up was the reason for all this, she was slowly battling the decision that overpowered her logic; now was as good a time as any to end things with Marcus and move forward. Desmond, if nothing else, had shown her that her life was much fuller with someone who had passion. She struggled with the decision to try or not to try. As she picked up her luggage and entered the airport shuttle, she reflected on her current circumstances. *You're not happy, girl. It's time to end things, even if you can't be with Des. I want this trial separation to be permanent.* She began to practice what she would say to Marcus once she saw him. 'Marcus, I love you, but I'm not in love with you.' *No, it's too cliché.* 'Marcus, I'm not in love with you.' *No, that was too blunt* for a man she'd known so long. 'It's over, Marcus. I'm sorry.' That sounded uninspired.

"Lady, who are you talking to?" the shuttle driver asked.

"Excuse me?"

"You keep saying it 'I'm sorry, Marcus,' but there's no one left on this shuttle but you and me. I was just wondering who you were talking to."

"Oh, sorry, I'm just practicing something."

"It sounds like a break-up."

It was somewhat embarrassing to be caught by the shuttle diver, but she was emotionally drained by everything. She ultimately resigned herself to her emotions. She was in total conflict, and completely unsure how Marcus would take the news of her being out of the country and establishing a relationship with a new man. A man she wasn't even sure she could have a relationship with. New Orleans wasn't far from Houston, and if he actually got a job in automotive engineering, there were several companies in Houston that would need someone like him. The more she thought about it, the more confused she became. It was true she had feelings for Marcus, and he showed a desire to change. To grow. It was more than he had shown in so very long. A year ago, it would have been all he ever needed to show. Promise. But now things were different. She was different. She'd never connected with him the way she did Desmond. Outside of liberating her sexually, he understood her quirks. He valued her, and she appreciated him. The truth of the matter was she was in love with him, and even his profession didn't bother her as long as he ended that chapter of his life, just as she was willing to end this chapter of her life. Marcus moving to Houston was a nonstarter. It was simply too late to salvage things with him. As the shuttle pulled up to her

184

car, she gathered her belongings and put them outside, where the driver kindly put them in the trunk of her car as she searched for change. 2-3 whls? Isn't car dead? Hasn't been driven

"Have a good day, miss," the gentleman said. Kendra nodded in kind. She was too preoccupied to think of anything else but how she left things with Desmond. It was time to go home and start moving her life forward. As she got in the car, she thought about calling Desmond again, but instead decided to concentrate on what she was going to say to Marcus. The drive was about thirty-five minutes away, enough time to practice her speech. She thought about the times they had before, and how much he cared about her. She thought about Desmond's words—maybe all this was a fantasy, and she was just caught up in the emotional high. She thought about how Mr. Baptiste touched her. She could never go back to what she considered normal. This was the new her, and as she pulled into the neighborhood, she stopped the car to take a look at the home that she and Marcus had shared over the last few years. It was her home as much as his. She understood that. But it was all he had. She loved him enough to make it easy on him. There would be no fight over the home. There would be no fight over anything. This was their final goodbye before she went to Houston. She parked the car and walked toward the house.

A lone voice stopped her.

"Excuse me... Kendra?" She turned around, a tall, red-haired Caucasian lady now standing in front of her. She looked like she'd been crying at some point in time.

"I'm sorry. Who are you?"

"It's Elaine."

"Who?"

"Of course you don't remember me. Elaine Holt."

"I'm sorry, that doesn't ring a bell."

Kendra walked off without a word, until Elaine dashed in front of her to resume the conversation.

"I used to work with Marcus when we were in the military."

"Okay, so what are you doing outside my house?"

"It's his house actually," she said with a smugness Kendra didn't like.

"So, I'm going to ask again. Who in the fuck are you and what are you doing outside my house?"

She stood there, waiting for a response as Elaine slipped her hand into her purse. A motion that made her senses slightly uneasy.

[handwritten note in margin: Taser? or gun? what you got bitch?]

"The thing is, and he and I didn't want you to find out this way, but we've been seeing each other. It started out as counseling, but it's evolved into something more. I just thought, woman to woman, I'd tell you that he's moving on with me."

Kendra examined the woman's face. The red hair filled her with certain venom.

"So, have you been fucking him in my house?"

"I've been fucking him everywhere."

"But did you fuck him in my house?"

"I fuck him all the time. My house, his car, I've even fucked him once or twice in a hospital. He wants to be with me. I'm the one there for him and you've been in the way of true love for too long. I'm sick of it. Marcus is sick of it. We both think it's time for you to move on."

The words ignited Kendra. She was upset and wanted to respond, but her instincts insisted she remained level headed. She began walk closer to the woman who tightened her grip on her purse.

"I'll be honest Elle"

"It's Elaine."

"Whatever, I'm not sure why Marcus wouldn't just tell me this hims—"

"He doesn't owe you anything. He's tired of you not being there for him."

"Is that right?"

"Yes that's right. There's nothing here for you."

Kendra examined the woman. It was certainly the woman Marcus had been sleeping with, the red hair confirmed as much, yet she seemed desperate. Her story didn't seem to add up entirely and she was obviously hiding something. She decided to use a disarming technique Marcus had taught her.

"Elaine...it's fine. You're right. You can have him. Tell Marcus to send me my things... I'll be leaving."

"Wait... you're leaving?"

"Yeah this is nonsense. I'm not going to fight over a man."

"He's not just any man."

"You're right. He's yours...all yours."

Kendra sunk her head as Elaine finally removed her hand from her purse to comfort her.

"We're both so sorry Kendra. We didn't want you to find out this way. It's just that we're in lo—"

Wham! Kendra delivered a bruising right jab to Elaine's esophagus. The former corporal fell to her knees, and her eyes watered instantly. The purse slid onto the ground, exposing a 22 caliber pistol Elaine was evidently holding onto. Kendra walked over to pick up the gun.

Ha! No more deep throut for ya!

"See, I thought you were bat shit crazy... I think I'll hold onto this gun."

Wham! she hit her again.

As she was on the ground, Kendra continued the conversation.

"Listen, you redheaded bitch, I'm not sure what Marcus told you, but the old me who would've sat here and been reasonable and tried to understand what you were saying left a long time ago. I asked you a question—were you fucking in my house?"

Wham! Kendra hit her a third time and the woman could barely breathe. She looked at her, gasping for air.

"You know what? It doesn't matter. I'm going to go in there and deal with *your* man. After that, I'm gonna come back out here, and if you are on my property when I get back, I'm going to take my time and mop your ass up and down this street like the useless home-wrecking cunt you are." Kendra looked at Elaine on the ground and kicked her in the ribs as hard as she could, then headed into the house.

When she opened the door, she went straight to the closet in the foyer and pulled out a long, black, aluminum bat. She walked into the living room where Marcus was coming to greet her.

"KD! Hey, baby, how was your—"

He couldn't finish his sentence. Kendra swung the bat upwards, connecting with the testicles, forcing Marcus to crumble onto the ground in agonizing pain. *Oh shit!*

"Hello, Marcus. Don't get up. My trip was fine. In fact, I spent the majority of it on my back getting turned into a stone-cold freak. But I guess that's something you know all too well, since I just met the red-headed white bitch you've been screwing in our house for God knows how long. She took the bat and hit him across the back. He fell hard.

"Kendra! Baby wait! You're making a terrible—" *mistake!? How?*

She pulled the gun she took from Elaine and pointed it towards him.

"I don't want to hear your lying ass speak."

"But I can expla—" *why?*

Pop! She pulled the trigger of the gun, nearly hitting him. He began to tremble, something which surprised her since he'd made a living *fear or tremors* being shot at, but she could tell he was in excruciating pain from being hit in his scrotum. Pulling the trigger again was beyond tempting, but her message was received, she had his undivided attention.

"You know, I'm glad this happened because I was honestly torn about staying with your ass or trying to move on with my life, but now it's all too clear. You've been fucking around since Houston, and we both know it. And life is way too short to be unhappy. You can have this place and everything in it. You can take that tramp outside and fuck her until Christ returns for all I care. I'm out of here. Don't call or contact me, you unfaithful piece of shit. It's over!" *What about your stuff? Leaving everything behind*

"Kendra! Baby please! I need to tell yo—"

"It's over! Stay the fuck away from me!"

With those words, Kendra turned around, taking the bat and pistol with her and proceeding to the car. She scanned the area to see if Elaine was anywhere near her property. She wasn't. She walked back toward the car and got in the vehicle, quickly backing out. A tear fell from her eye as she used her phone to make the only call that made any sense at the moment.

"This is Milton."

"Milton, hi, this is Kendra Daniels. How are you?"

"My world is much better now that you're on the phone. What can I do for you?"

Kendra stopped at the stop sign and wiped a final tear from her eye as she looked back at the house she had been living in. A house she had grown to love as her own.

"I'm taking the job in Houston." *Closer to her new man Avonis own*

188

THINGS REMEMBERED

"You have to move on, Desmond," he said aloud while sitting in the park waiting on a client. It was a lie he'd been telling himself over and over since leaving Saint Martin. So much of his life had changed in the past few weeks. He thought about his time with Kendra, mainly. He hoped she was doing okay. Still regretting his decision, he looked at his phone. He wanted to call her, but knew his job would get in the way. She deserved better than him, even if she didn't know it. He shifted on the bench as he anticipated his client. *Where is she?* It wasn't long before she was sitting next to him on the park bench holding two cups of green tea from Starbucks. As a courtesy, Desmond reluctantly took one from her hand.

"Hi."

"Well, hello, Desmond. How was your trip?"

"We need to talk."

"About what exactly?"

"I'm out of the business, effective immediately." The woman shifted her weight on the park bench, raising her eyebrows as if to indicate she was stunned by his statement.

"Congratulations. Must have been a hell of a trip. I'm a little confused, though. What does that have to do with me since we've never had sex?"

"You know damn well what it means."

"Well, I have to say I'm genuinely happy for you. Retirement is always a good thing. We should throw you a party. But in the meantime, give me what I need and you can be on your merry way."

"I can't do that."

The woman took a sip of her tea. She placed it on the bench next to her.

"You know, when I met you, you were just this charming waiter who, I'll admit, had a little swagger. You were bold—bold to the point that you tried to get my phone number, which was cute, so I gave it to you. When you called, you realized that I never intended to date you. I was just trying to introduce you to Anita."

"What's your point?"

"My point is, that when you met Anita, you thought you were about to live every man's wet dream—the ol' two-for-one special. That is, until you realized that Anita, your former boss, my college dorm mate, was an aspiring pimp, and I was passing you along for a small finder's fee. It was then that it hit you—you were being turned out. You thought you had a chance with me, but you didn't realize you were out of your league. As far as you saying you can't give me what I came here for, you certainly can and will, because this is your crushing reality, Desmond. Once again, you don't realize you're simply out of your league."

Desmond looked at her. She may have been right, but so was he.

"This isn't right."

"It's not a matter of right and wrong—it's a matter of professionalism."

"Can't we just—"

"Desmond, I'd like to tell you a story. A man walked into a bar and met a woman who he thought was very attractive. He made several advances to her, all of which she refused. After a while, the man asked, 'What if I gave you a million dollars to sleep with me tonight?' The woman was shocked. She'd never seen a million dollars and wasn't sure what to do. In her hesitation, the man changed his offer and said,

'What if I gave you ten dollars?' The woman, offended, responded, 'Ten dollars? What kind of woman do you think I am?' The man responded, 'We've already established what kind of woman you are. Now we're just negotiating.' I say that to say this. You're the kind of whore whose price is fifty-thousand dollars. I hired you for your professionalism. I hired you for your discretion. And above all, I hired you to do a job and walk away unattached because that's what whores do."

His anger bubbled over. He thought about getting up and walking away. Instead, he hesitated, curling his fist into a ball as if to force the pressure back into his body. The woman smiled. "You know what? You're right, Desmond, you don't have to do this. Any of it. Let's call the whole thing off." She stood up and took two steps away from the bench. "You can have the moral high ground. Try this ridiculous attempt at growing a conscience and save the girl. Delete the flash drive with all your sorted details of a good time in a tropical island, or you can take the fifty-thousand dollars. I'm offering to pay for your sister's medical bills. Breast cancer, isn't it? Stage two?"

"Fuck you, Ronnie,"

"Oh, honey, even with the fifty thousand I'm giving you, you could never afford this pussy."

Desmond handed her the flash drive, a catalog of video files containing the sexual and questionable things he had done on the island with Kendra. In exchange, he took the envelope out of her hand, frustrated with his choices. He began to count the money. He knew it was all there. He just wanted to make sure she knew he didn't trust her. When he was done running his fingers through the bills, he heard Ronnie speak.

"Satisfied?"

He wasn't. The money was in order, but he wasn't satisfied with himself. Not with what he was doing as a way to pay his sister's medical bills, and most importantly, what he had done to Kendra. Recording all their encounters and passing the info along to Ronnie Duvalle for cash was an easy job until he met Kendra and subsequently fell in love with her. Everything he had just been a part of left a rancid feeling in the pit of his stomach. He wanted to know more.

"Why are you doing this to her?"

"Me? Let's be very clear. I did nothing—you did this to her." A final blow that confirmed his betrayal.

"Why do you hate her?"

"I don't hate her, at all. In fact, I actually like the woman, about as much as you do. Enough to treat her with compassion and friendship and support, but not enough to let her get in the way of my work. This is a competition, and I hate competition."

"She's not a threat... to whatever you got going on. She just wants to be happy. Move to a big city and be happy."

"And how do you know what is and what isn't a threat in my life, Desmond? Such a pretty face with no brain whatsoever. I can see how she'd be attracted to you. Here's a startling reality—she's a woman with ambition, and there's nothing more dangerous in this world."

"She's not going to get in your way. She thinks you're friends."

"Then I will never need to use the information on this flash drive against her."

"I just think—"

"Desmond, I'd love to talk, but, well, I honestly don't give a damn about your opinion, so it's a waste of time for both of us. It's been a pleasure doing business with you."

Desmond got up and walked away. Of all his times sleeping with women for money, this one transaction—his biggest payday—made him feel more sleazy than all the rest. He tried to remind himself why he was doing what he did. He looked for his sister's number in his phone and pressed 'Call'.

"Hello."

"Teri? It's Des."

"I know who it is. My breasts are sick, not my ears, little bro." It was her way of breaking the ice. Teri was always the type to address the elephant in the room at any given moment.

"Well, it's funny you say that 'cause—"

"It's funny I have breast cancer?"

"No, that's not what I meant. I—"

"Then what were you going to say, Des? 'Cause you're sounding like an asshole, right now."

"No, Teri, I was—"

"You were trying to do what? I'm fighting for my life over here, and you're being insensitive. I haven't even heard from you in three weeks. It's like you just... don't... care..." *He at here holy for you!*

There were sobs from the other end of the phone. Desmond held it speechless. He didn't know what to say.

"Teri, I'm... sorry."

"Des..."

"Yeah?"

"Are you ever gonna stop being a bitch?"

His sister howled on the other end of the phone. She was sick, it was true, but she never hesitated to play a joke on her little brother.

"Damn it, Teri, quit joking around. That wasn't funny."

"Oh, it was funny as shit! You should've heard your voice cracking. I haven't heard you sound like that since you were sixteen! Lil bitch."

She laughed again. As always, he was the punchline in her joke. But it felt good to hear his sister laugh. He decided to get in on the banter.

"Well, ha ha ha, motherfucker, very funny," he responded, trying to break up the laughter. "But that's kind of what I wanted to talk to you about."

"What are you talking about, Des?"

"I need you to do me a favor."

"See, this is why you don't answer the phone for family. Soon as they call, they need a favor. Well, let's hear it. What do you need?"

"Call Doctor Kegan and set up the second round of chemo. I have the money—all of it. Get whatever you need. We're going to fight this together." *Despicable they want treat w/o payment!*

There were no false sobs this time around. His sister muffled the phone in tears. He stopped in his tracks and fought back tears of his own. After several sobs, his sister finally asked, "Des, how did you—?"

"Don't worry about that. It was nothing illegal. I told you I would handle it, and I did."

"Des, I don't know what to say. I just can't—"

"Teri, you have taken care of me since I was twelve. You taught me almost everything I know, most important of which is how to look out for a person and be a man of your word. When I say I got you, I

So who taught you to lie to women?

193

got you. Now, call Doctor Kegan. I'll have the money to the hospital tomorrow."

His sister wept through the phone. After a few deep breaths, she responded, "I love you, Des. You still a lil bitch, but I love you."

"I love you too, sis. Now call Doctor Kegan."

He disconnected the phone. A tear fell from his eye as he thought about all his transgressions. He was a whore, there was no denying it, and he had done something terrible to someone he loved. He was a hypocrite for telling her she deserved better when he hadn't been better, but he had done what needed to be done for his family. Kendra made him feel like a king, but she wasn't his sister. More importantly, she wasn't going to choose him as bad as he wanted her to. Ronnie was right about one thing: women like that were simply out of his league. He'd never see her again, as bad as he wanted to be with her at this very moment. She was the first person in this world to see the light in him. To recognize he was a man who was more than his profession. It didn't matter; none of it mattered. He had a job to do, and he did it. And Kendra, she was going to patch up her life with Marcus.

It was time to move on. As he cleared his head about his newly defunct lover, his phone rang. Assuming it was his big sister telling him she talked to Doctor Kegan, he answered without checking the ID.

"Hello?"

"Hi." The voice on the other end was one he had grown to love over the last few weeks.

"Hi."

"I just broke up with Marcus. I want to be with you, Des. Can we talk?"

Of course you will

Oh shit! Not to mention she gonna be prego

BE SURE TO READ RONNIE: A MONEY, POWER & SEX STORY, too. And remember, all things come to a head in MONEY, POWER & SEX II: THE SCENT OF DECEIT coming soon!

ABOUT THE AUTHOR

Norian Love was born in Los Angeles, California, in 1979. He grew up in Houston, Texas, where he's lived for the last twenty years. While taking a short hiatus from working for Fortune 500 companies as a technology specialist, he rediscovered his passion for writing poetry and released his first book, *Theater of Pain*, which was critically acclaimed. The reception and momentum of this book sparked him to create his eagerly anticipated follow-up, *Games of the Heart*, a few years later. The final installment of his poetic trilogy, *The Dawn or the Dusk,* was also a critical success. He released *Money, Power & Sex: A Love Story*, his first novel, in April of 2016 to critical acclaim.

Feb 2023

Marcus 2/7.

Gibson 2/14

Ronnie 2/28

Savkaryant 2/21

MPS 2: Scent of Deceit

If you enjoyed this book or found it useful, I'd be very grateful if you'd post a short review on Amazon. Your support really does make a difference, and I read all the reviews personally, so I can get your feedback and make this book even better.

If you'd like to leave a review, then all you need to do is click the review link on this book's page on Amazon: Click to Write a Review

Thanks again for your support!

Kendra Daniels — back in VA, demotion   with marcus — slept ō
dark skinned   Pre calc Kendra — nickname M college   Ronnie in Haz
5'-4"   had braces
curvy   P 49 doesnt want kids

Booked FLIGHT to St Marth.

P113 pussy passport got stamped

P173 6 years together

Ronnie Duvalle — Burrows Industries — Haston based
                        caller ID : Queen Savage Bitch p 2
P54 patron — her favorite drink   Lp38 Name change to Ronnie

Nichelle Myers — replaced Kendra @ the company
                took leave of absence
                Broke up w/ Lucas when he got shot by cops

Andrew
2/6/23

Target
stock : 110J 15→ n→ 16½

Serseant Marcus Winters – Army   Bravo Company – p 43
   supposed to be Kendra's man but... fucked Ronnie   p11
   fucking [Elaine] Holt red head (chpt 2)   5'7" blue eyes
p109   └ supposed to be his military counselor!   p 40 Fake boobs
9 inches!   paid off home with GI bill

p 21   dropped a drink!   p 46 2nd time dropped a drink
                        └ stroke? arm weakness?
   p 110 seizure after blow job w/ Elaine   (P 177)
   p 176 dx w/ rare form of Parkinsons   (2-5 years to)
                                         (live)

         - p190 waiter, pimped out by Anitta – Ronnie's
                                    College roommate
Desmond Baptiste 6-3 St martin   Fuck Boi!
   From New orleans
   p 70 Georgia Tech – Degree in automotive engineering
                                           - medical bills
   P 191 paid $50,000 by Ronnie! Sister Teri has breast ca

                  went to afghanistan   cut his wrists
Ryan Hayes - Bravo Company tried to take his life on P92
white   suicide watch at VA hospital
          P 92 calls Marcus "GI Negro" LMAO
     P 93   Likes to drink 1929 macallan — whiskey

notes: Elaine doesn't clean, doesn't cook, talks too much p142
       └ white, red head   └ everyday sex-101

P 162 "This wasn't for the sport, but rather the spirit," Ooh! Fire!
  "Dorian"

51 Use whats App to tullc for free in the islands!
6 Rainbow pussy, you got this!
1 Let one of those Caribbean mandingo's drill a hole in your back
34 Youre a goddamn unicorn sitting on a pussy made of rainbows

names for it

- p10 vessel
- p10 dick
- p11 penis
- p11 rod
- p47 package
- p47 member

Made in United States
North Haven, CT
21 December 2022

29971878R00114